*P*A MODERN DAY *ersuasion*

An Adaptation of Jane Austen's Classic

by Kaitlin Saunders

ISBN: 1439261172
ISBN-13: 9781439261170
LCCN: 2009910582

This book is dedicated to

my mother, who always believed in

me and introduced me to my first love,

the works of Jane Austen.

Prologue

March 19, 2001

The world was over for seventeen year old Anne Elliot. With tears streaming down her face, she lay crying on her bed, clutching a pillow which was now drenched with tears. Anne's beautifully appointed bedroom, which normally was a treasured haven, now seemed more like a prison than a place of rest, a place holding her captive from the man she loved. Glancing up, Anne spotted her godmother Carol Russell, her mother's most trusted friend, looking beseechingly at her. Carol was unsuccessfully trying to make Anne understand that this decision was in her best interest. Usually, time spent with Carol brought a feeling of security and a sense of well being to Anne. When Anne's mother died, Carol assumed the role of surrogate mother, loving Anne as she would her own daughter. Now reaching out to Anne with empathy, Carol attempted to hug the distraught and weeping girl, but the gesture was quickly rejected. Carol's comforting embrace this time held no solace for Anne. How could the arms of a friend ever compare to the embrace of one's soul mate? Still, Carol did her best to placate the heartbroken Anne, despite the rejection.

Anne recognized the hurt in Carol's eyes. She hated that she was treating Carol this way, knowing full well that her actions were causing pain to the older woman. Even in

Anne's torturous agony, Anne still had compassion for others, a character trait that her own mother, Emma Elliot, had treasured in her daughter. She used to tell Anne she could have been the 'poster child' of every parent's dreams: effortless to raise, ready to please, and consistently obedient to a fault. But at this moment Anne did not appreciate these qualities in herself. Her eagerness to please now could only be viewed as a curse!

Neither her father nor Carol had approved of Rick, a handsome young man of 20, whom Anne had met the summer before. She remembered the day vividly. Her older sister Elizabeth had cajoled her into a game of tennis at the country club, attended by only the rich and privileged. Afterwards, Anne wanted to celebrate her win with a cooling dip in the pool. Her sister readily agreed but for a different reason. Elizabeth was eager to meet the new lifeguard she had heard so much about. Rumors were circulating that he was quite easy on the eyes. As she watched Elizabeth smother her lips in gloss, Anne could not understand her sister's fixation with boys. The guys Elizabeth had brought home seemed obnoxious and really stuck on themselves. This lifeguard probably wasn't any different. After successfully coaxing her sister away from the mirror, Anne headed out to the pool, eager for a refreshing swim. Turning to ask Elizabeth a question, she realized that her flighty sister had already disappeared. Sweeping the area, Anne quickly spied Elizabeth making a beeline for the Lifeguard station. Aggravated, Anne rolled her eyes in frustration, exasperated at all the havoc this one guy was causing.

Gazing up to the lifeguard stand, Anne decided to see what all the hype was about. There, before her, sat a tall, suntanned young man with piercing blue eyes and a magnificently built frame. Although handsome, his features weren't perfect by any means, having a bit too much of a Roman nose. Still, there was something about his appearance which struck Anne to the core. To her embarrassment,

Anne realized she too was gawking at his sheer manliness. The reversed phrase 'Me Jane, You Tarzan' popped into her head. Blinking her eyes to get a grip on reality, she chided herself and began to laugh at her silliness. Determined not to give this guy a bigger head than he must already have, she purposely decided to ignore him. Wrenching her eyes away, she tossed off her flip-flops and sunglasses to quickly execute what she hoped would be a perfect dive into the pool. However, in her hurry to 'ignore' the new lifeguard, she inadvertently tripped over a pile of stacked ropes used to divide pool sections. To her horror, she found herself hitting the water with a painful belly flop.

If that had been the worst of it, only her ego and stomach would have been bruised. But unfortunately, Anne discovered that both an ankle and her right arm were entangled in the ropes. Her frantic struggle to free herself only caused further entrapment. Instinctually, she panicked, yelling out for help. Within seconds, Anne found herself being rescued by Rick Wentworth, the new lifeguard, a young man who, at that moment, became her 'knight-in-shining-armor'. She took one look into his concerned face and knew he had captured her heart. Later, Elizabeth accused her of tripping on purpose, which Anne vehemently denied. *No,* thought Anne pensively, she was certain it could only have been fate.

But now fate was causing Anne to do 'the right thing' and please her elders rather than herself. It only took one disapproving glance from either Carol or her father to make her capitulate rather than witness their displeasure. Anne feared that if she did not follow their advice to the letter, it would surely ruin her life...and Anne was never one to take risks.

Now, here was Carol telling the agitated and distressed Anne the right choice had been made. Was it only hours ago that her father had found Anne packing her suitcase? Carol had rushed over when Walter Elliot placed his desperate call for help, telling Carol an 'emergency' situation had sprung up. What her father assumed was a silly crush had ended in a marriage proposal! Her father considered Rick beneath them socially. This alone made the young man entirely unsuitable for an 'Elliot'. After all, Rick was not fortunate enough to have been born into an affluent family and had no hopes of receiving any kind of inheritance. To Walter, these facts made it clear Rick was a worthless nobody and certainly not an eligible suitor for Anne. Mr. Elliot further assumed that Rick was most likely working at the club with the ambition to get his hands on some heiress' money. Walter was adamant it would *not* be his daughter who fell victim, and Mrs. Russell was in complete agreement. Carol equally had been sure the summer romance would fizzle out. Although she had noticed Anne's slight blushes and increased visits to the fitness club, Carol felt the relationship would only be a passing fancy, especially for Rick, considering the many girls who were determined to supplant Anne. Carol was confident the novelty of Anne's hero worship would soon wear off and one of the more mature beauties at the club would replace the innocent Anne in his affections. Although Carol realized Anne would be crushed, in the end, it would be a good lesson for her. Anne was much too young to get involved and had far too much potential to be saddled to a loser. With all Anne had going for her, Carol knew that if steered in the right direction, she could quickly climb the ladder of success. The idea of Anne settling down with a mere boy who could offer her god-daughter nothing gave Carol nightmares. With Rick, the best Anne could hope for was a house full of children and a good-for-nothing husband barely putting food on the table. Most likely, Anne would have to work outside the home just to make ends meet. The thought caused Carol to shudder. Anne was far too precious to Carol for her to just sit back and allow this to happen. No, what Anne needed now was some good old-fashioned common sense and a healthy dose of reality! Carol felt it was her duty to persuade Anne out of this foolishness. Considering the promise Carol had made to Anne's mother only a few years earlier, she had no other option than to stop Anne from ruining her life. Of course, heartache would follow, but with time that would pass. Besides, Carol would be there to comfort Anne until a more suitable man came into Anne's life—a man from a socially upstanding family who could provide Anne with all the things she was accustomed to.

Anne, however, did not share this opinion. She felt more than ready to begin a life with Rick. What was money when they had love? Rick was a hard worker, and with her beside him, Anne felt certain they would conquer the world. But despite all of Anne's well-rehearsed appeals, neither her father nor Carol would budge. Steadfastly, they held to the conviction that Rick was simply using her to gain access to the Elliot fortune. When they said as much to Rick's face, he blew up with anger, telling them in forceful terms that he could care less about their disgusting money. He only wanted Anne.

It was then that her father made a proposition. Allow Anne to graduate from college first, and then he would reconsider Rick's proposal.

"That's at least four years!" gasped Rick.

With pleading eyes, Rick told Anne to make a choice… either him or college. She hesitated, torn. Surely, she could please *both* her father and Rick? If she chose college, perhaps Rick would be willing to wait? But Rick wasn't waiting. When he saw Anne's indecision, Rick turned on his heels, slamming the door behind him. With numbing shock, she watched him exit, feeling as if her very heart had been ripped from her body. *How can accepting the advice of my father and Carol rather than following my heart feel so wrong?*

The sound of a vehicle starting in the driveway disrupted Anne's thoughts. She rushed to the window, feeling certain that with Rick leaving, so was her future. Looking towards the street with her vision clouded by tears, Anne still managed to watch Rick as he backed his old, rusty truck out of her father's driveway. She pounded on the window as hard as she could, yelling for Rick to stay—but he couldn't hear her.

Mrs. Russell pulled her away from the window. "Anne, stop this!" implored Carol. Devastated, Anne collapsed onto the bed with even more heart wrenching sobs.

Rick sat in his truck, taking one last longing look at Anne's room. Not seeing her, he squealed off into the night...bitterness filling his veins.

Over seven years later...

"Anne, are you listening?" Carol stared at the pleasant faced young woman currently engaged in daydreaming. The two were in the middle of a consultation in Carol's upscale office to critique Anne's latest card designs.

Carol's suite was clean and orderly. Her spacious and impressive mahogany desk held an opened laptop where photo's of the Elliot family could be seen. The walls of Carol's office were filled with modern artwork created by local artists and on either side of the room were stunning floor to ceiling windows which showcased beautiful downtown Portland, Oregon. Both women sat at a gorgeous coffee table made from a huge redwood having a diameter of over 30 inches. On its smooth lacquered surface lay a multitude of Anne's card designs, along with price perspectives in addition to Carol's handwritten notes.

Anne, now 25, had a sweet demeanor about her, being blessed with a smile that showed her gentle heart. She had soft features and long, silky, deep brown hair which she usually pulled back into a bun. Her eyes, a vivid shade of olive green, were big and expressive, but their impact was diminished by a deep sadness harboring within. Her beauty was quiet and reminded Carol of a flower just waiting to blossom if only love would awaken its heart. Anne was not flashy or commercialized...she was just...Anne. Strangers often thought she had been trained in ballet, as Anne's posture was impeccable and she held herself in such a graceful manner. Carol often remarked of the resemblance between Anne and her mother, something which pleased her god-daughter.

"Sorry," said Anne, blushing as she shuffled through the designs to disguise being caught in a moment of reflection.

Anne found her passion in creating quaint greeting cards which Carol sold in the teashop she owned in downtown Portland. Anne's latest line was dubbed 'Words from the Heart' which featured calligraphy and hand drawn designs. Her other successful creations included picturesque home greeting cards, vibrant pressed flowers and dresses cut from assorted chic fabrics.

"What were you thinking about?" inquired Carol. As much as Carol liked the new designs, she was more curious to find out why Anne seemed so distracted.

Anne stopped, trying to decide whether to tell Carol what was truly on her mind. Anne did not always agree with Carol's advice, but she knew that whatever wisdom Carol imparted would be seasoned with genuine love. Her godmother had always sought only the best for her, so Anne decided to take a chance, asking, "Do you ever wish that things had turned out differently? I mean, life-wise?"

Carol continued to make notes on Anne's designs. "Certainly. I wish my husband had not died. I wish many things. But dear…we can't live in the past."

Anne looked down in sadness, "But, do you regret some of the decisions you've made? Do you ever think about what might have been?"

"I…" Carol paused, giving Anne her full attention now. She knew Anne well enough to sense this was not a general question.

Taking time to study Anne, Carol saw before her an accomplished young woman full of creative talent. A graduate from Willamette University at the top of her class with a Bachelor's in Business, Anne had unlimited promise. Too much so to be dredging up the past and living with regrets.

If her suspicions were right, Carol knew what Anne was referring to. "Please, tell me this is not what I think it is—"

"Yes," Anne interjected with slight defiance, "I can't help but believe if I had only married Rick we would have been happy together."

"But there's no certainty in that, dear," Carol said calmly. "When he proposed, you still had two months of high school to complete and had recently been awarded the scholarship to Willamette. What did Rick have? Just a high school diploma and no career to speak of. Most likely you would have needed to drop out of school to help make ends meet and—"

"But if we were in love..." interrupted Anne.

Carol paused and looked tenderly at Anne, "Sweetheart, love doesn't pay the bills. Besides, if he'd really been in love, Rick would have stuck around to gain your dad's approval, even if it took years. He also wouldn't have left you hanging all this time with not even a word, now would he?"

The words cut deep and Carol regretted speaking so bluntly. Carol lovingly pressed her hand sympathetically on Anne's in an attempt to soften the painful truth. Even though Anne did her best to mask her anguish, the wounds inflicted that cold March day seven long years ago were still with Anne as if it were yesterday, and hearing what Carol just said made the agony cut deeper.

"Come on, you have so much on the ball now, you certainly don't need to be pining away for some immature boy who had no future. It's time to move on and let things lie in the past. I'm sure Rick has." Anne forced a fake smile and nodded, satisfying Carol who was ready to get back to business. "Now, about this design. It's particularly good. I was thinking I'll send this off to my friend at Hallmark today."

Chapter 1

Anne reveled in weekends like this, having the house all to herself. Her father and older sister Elizabeth were out of town touring Napa Valley, and they weren't expected to return until Monday. Turning on her stereo, Anne allowed the music to swell loudly throughout the house, simply enjoying the freedom to do so. She sighed with contentment as she sat in the refuge of her bedroom composing a letter.

She loved her room with its comfy full bed blanketed by a hand-made quilt. Sitting at a small desk situated in front of a window, Anne peered out to appreciate the beautiful gardens below. Opening the window slightly, a fresh aroma of Daphne Odora encompassed her nostrils as she breathed in the delicate scent. Scanning her cherished haven, she noted the tall bookcase holding some of her most treasured books. On its shelves sat the works of great authors such as Jane Austen, Elizabeth Gaskell, Charles Dickens, and Beatrix Potter—all of which were Anne's favorites. Anne kept her room tidy, just like her life. It was her personal sanctuary, a place where, regardless whether others were home, she could find peace and solace. Her soft and inviting bed was perfectly situated next to a large bay window that overlooked the family's stately landscaped drive. Her room was spacious, well organized and perpetually smelled of freshly laundered sheets with a hint of lavender. To Anne's delight and joy, her room held a small cove area situated in the corner next to the walk-in closet. In its recesses, Anne found she could reveal her most deep and secret thoughts onto paper. It was also where the inspiration for the majority of Anne's card designs were created. Anne loved to curl up in the cushions with a good book or sit at her desk to keep up with correspondence. Her mother had helped Anne decorate this room just before becoming ill. The theme was pink and full of princesses. That was over ten years ago and even though Anne had outgrown such things, she didn't have the heart to change a single detail because it reminded Anne too much of her mother. This room was Anne's last connection to the woman who had so influenced her life. Sadly, her father had removed all other traces of Emma throughout the rest of the home. He did so to protect himself. It was his way of coping with the pain, as he too, had loved her mother very deeply. Seeing things which reminded him of Emma simply hurt him too much.

Anne thought back to when she was fourteen. Emma, their beautiful mother, had gathered her three daughters together: Elizabeth age fifteen; Anne; and Mary, age eleven; embracing each one as if to never let them go. With a calm voice she announced that she had cancer. The girls were devastated. Mary started to cry and Anne told her mother there must be a mistake. How could anyone so pretty as their mom be sick? Although Anne had noticed her mother's diminished weight and lack of energy, she never thought to question why. Emma sadly shook her head and with regret etched in her eyes, told them she only had a few weeks to live. The cancer, which had begun as a small cyst in their mother's knee, had spread to the lymph nodes, and then to her bones, and eventually to her lungs. Emma's eyes brimmed with unshed tears as she told them she was not afraid to die, however, the thought of leaving them behind was causing her immeasurable grief. Emma's sole concern was for her three precious girls. To leave them at the brink of womanhood seemed unthinkable and so unjust. Emma also knew her beloved husband would be in no state of mind after her death to care for them as they needed. Fortunately, Carol, her best friend since childhood, decided to locate closer in order to be near Emma until the end. With the move, Carol promised to look after the 'little Miss Elliot's', raising them as she would her own. Emma felt as if Carol was a godsend, for she knew her dear friend loved the girls almost as much as she did. This knowledge allowed Anne's mother to have peace during her final days, knowing her children were to be left in good hands.

Emma managed to live another ten months, bravely slipping away quietly, surrounded by the ones she loved most. The doctor was surprised, saying it must have been sheer will power that had kept their mother alive that long. Anne rejected the doctor's assumption. She knew it was love.

The intercom rang, indicating there was someone at the front door. Since Anne was not expecting anyone, she was half-tempted to pretend no one was at home but thought better of it. What if it was the friendly old lady next door needing some help again or Carol stopping by on her way home from work?

Anne hurried down the long staircase to the huge double doors. She peered through the peephole to see a messenger standing outside holding a large yellow envelope. Opening the door with caution, Anne left the chain lock in place. The messenger smiled, holding up an electronic slate for Anne's signature, passing it through the cracked door. Anne signed off and thanked the messenger as he handed the envelope in return.

Closing the door, she looked oddly at the package. It was addressed to Mr. Elliot and said, 'Immediate Response Requested', bearing a return address of Shepherd, Zielinski & Steinburg, Attorneys at Law. Knowing it could be important, and also that her father wouldn't object, Anne decided to open it.

Even in her wildest dreams, Anne could not have imagined what she read. The papers held a notification of a foreclosure on their home! She wondered at first if this was some sort of joke, but quickly realized the court seal was authentic, along with official documentation from their bank. A thought popped up unbidden into Anne's head—*No wonder he left town*! She chided herself for thinking badly of her father, but yet was resentful at having to face this alone. How quickly things change! Wasn't it only ten minutes earlier she had been thankful to have the house all to herself? Now, she couldn't wait for her family to return!

Chapter 2

Carol was a fashion plate. Despite being a widow for many years, she didn't let that hinder her from keeping up with designer trends or the social scene. Many admired Carol's ability to dress with class and flair. Her hair was an exquisite shade of silver, which was the envy of older women, and Carol kept it short, much like Judi Dench. Her trademark was to wear either black or brown, using color simply to accessorize. Anne thought her godmother a lovely woman and admired the way Carol always spoke her mind. Carol never had children of her own, but didn't feel cheated since the Elliot girls had filled that void, always making it her duty to guide and advise them. Of the three Elliot girls, she and Anne were the closest, forging a strong bond of love.

Carol sat looking at the foreclosure notice, "Has your dad seen this?"

Earlier that morning, upon receiving an S.O.S. call from Anne, she agreed to meet with her god-daughter at their favorite coffee shop. It was a little hole in the wall, but the coffee was exceptional. For a Saturday, it was especially busy, but luckily they had been able to secure a booth. Soft piano tunes played in the background, lending a relaxing aura to drown out the buzzing coffee grinders and chiming cash registers amongst the throng of people.

Anne shook her head negatively in reply to Carol's question, taking a sip of her steaming coffee before speaking. "Dad, Elizabeth, and Susan won't be in town until tomorrow."

Susan Clay was Elizabeth's friend. Anne didn't trust or care for her, feeling she was just looking for her next meal ticket after a recent divorce.

"What's your next course of action?" Carol asked.

"That's the $26,000 question," began Anne, "I don't know, move I guess. I can't touch my mother's estate for another five years. The thing that gets me is Dad didn't even tell me he was in financial trouble!"

Carol shrugged, "Maybe he didn't know."

Resentment showed in Anne's face. "That's hard for me to believe. More likely he didn't care." Anne took another sip of her coffee and wondered how tomorrow would play out with the return of her father and sister. She was not looking forward to it.

Chapter 3

Anne often dreamed about getting a place of her own, reveling in the thought of decorating and establishing herself as an individual—but she had yet to take that leap. After all, she was still considered a struggling artist, and until a company like Hallmark picked up her designs, she was not in a position to afford a place all by herself. At home, she was able to live rent free, and being a creature of habit, Anne didn't quite relish the thought of leaving her comfortable surroundings without a substantial reason other then simply wanting her own space. She was sensible, and content where she was. Other than some friction between Elizabeth and herself, Anne was pretty much free to do whatever she liked—that is, as long as dinner was on the table by six o'clock sharp.

Now, as Anne sat uncomfortably in the living room on the leather couch opposite her father's lawyer, Mr. Shepherd, she wished she had moved out long ago. Being at home obligated her to take part in family affairs she'd much rather avoid. Sighing, she looked at her watch. The two had been sitting in an awkward silence for nearly half an hour as they waited for her father's return.

Anne studied the aged face of Mr. Shepherd. He was her father's friend, having attended the same university as Mr. Elliot. Their friendship went way back, and Anne was glad Mr. Shepherd wasn't easily fooled by her eccentric father.

Hearing a honk outside, Anne looked out the window to see an unfamiliar red convertible pull into the driveway. In the car sat Mr. Elliot, Elizabeth, and Susan. Anne glanced at Mr. Shepherd with raised eyebrows as she rose to head outside to greet them.

"Oh, hello, Anne!" Mr. Elliot said as he caught sight of his daughter approaching.

Anne couldn't help but admire her father's well-kept frame and appearance. Mr. Elliot was still a fine looking man and reminded many of an older Cary Grant. He had a way about him, something that set him apart from others. Her dad still walked with confidence in his step—that indefinable charisma which shouted wealth and status. In his mid-sixties, he could still keep up with the best of them, taking great pride in his appearance. His manly features and well-toned figure made him quite sought after by the ladies. Walter was aware of his effect on the weaker sex, so much so, it seemed to him an everyday event to have the admiration of women. Even so, everyone was sure Walter would never remarry. Mr. Elliot had never really gotten over losing his Emma, plus, his inflated ego convinced him no one could ever compliment his looks the way his late wife had.

Anne turned to her sister in greeting, but to her dismay, Elizabeth didn't even bother to pause in her conversation with Susan to acknowledge her. Anne wondered why slights like this still managed to affect her. Anne and Elizabeth had never gotten along, though not due to any failings on Anne's part. Anne had always been kind and supportive, but Elizabeth chose to shut her out. Anne couldn't understand why. Elizabeth had it all. She was the beauty of the family and drop dead gorgeous. If one could win the lottery in face and form, she'd be hand's down the winner, having received the best genes from both her parents. Everywhere Elizabeth went, she caught the eyes of strangers. Her sister had dark expressive eyes and European features. As such, Elizabeth was the darling of their father—but oddly enough to Anne, it seemed that Elizabeth was jealous of her. Perhaps it was because people remarked that Anne reminded them so much of Emma.

Mr. Elliot motioned proudly to the car. "Isn't she a beauty? A 1955 convertible...just couldn't pass her up." He stood back and admired it. Anne couldn't pretend to be happy about it under the present circumstances.

"Dad," Anne said, "Mr. Shepherd is waiting for you inside." The tone in Anne's voice caused Elizabeth to send Mr. Elliot a questioning look. As Anne watched Elizabeth's reaction, she wondered how this news would affect her sister. Elizabeth made it a ritual to visit salons weekly to touch up her roots (she wasn't a natural blonde), receive rejuvenating facials, and enjoy frequent manicures and pedicures. Not only that, three times a week, she met with a personal trainer. Elizabeth looked like money, having exquisite taste and it was *always* expensive. She spared nothing when it came to her appearance. To Elizabeth, it was her prize possession. Unfortunately, the maintaining of her beauty was time consuming and never allowed her sister to really find out what she could truly offer the world. Sadly, after people met Elizabeth, the only thing they could recall were her looks. It was the only thing that defined her.

Intrigued by curiosity, Elizabeth and Susan went inside, followed by a rather hesitant Mr. Elliot. Anne was left standing alone with only the forgotten suitcases. Sighing, she picked up what she could carry and headed indoors.

Anne arrived just in time to hear Mr. Shepherd deliver the news. The room became deathly silent. Elizabeth sat in shock and Susan looked uncomfortable, wishing to escape this awkward situation. All eyes were on Mr. Elliot as they waited for his reply. Walter had stationed himself in front of the large bay window overlooking the well-kept backyard and pool, not uttering a word since Mr. Shepherd announced the reason for his visit.

Breaking the silence, he turned and looked at Mr. Shepherd with disbelief. "File for bankruptcy?" Mr. Shepherd nodded affirmatively, pulling some papers out of his brief-case. Mr. Elliot turned to Anne, "Anne, did you know about this?" he asked.

Anne nodded and took a seat. "The foreclosure notice came on Friday."

"Well, I must say I am quite surprised!" he said as he sat down.

Mr. Shepherd shot Anne an exasperated look. "Really? I don't see how that's possible. I've been sending you notices for weeks."

Mr. Elliot looked between Anne and Mr. Shepherd sheepishly. "Come on, Shepherd—" he pleaded.

Mr. Shepherd's demeanor remained unchanged. "There's nothing I can do to get you out of this one, Walter."

"What do you suggest we do then?" Elizabeth asked.

"The only plausible option is to do exactly what I've been recommending…get legal protection to keep what assets you have, and then sell everything else." Mr. Shepherd's advice shocked Mr. Elliot.

"Everything! Even the new convertible?"

"Yes, Walter, even the car. But to be honest, the convertible is the least of your worries," said Mr. Shepherd.

Elizabeth whitened. "It's that bad? But what about my stuff? Will I have to give up my car, too?"

Taking pity on Elizabeth's frightened face, Mr. Shepherd answered, "There's no need for you to panic. Anything that is in your name, including your Mercedes, is safe. Now, regarding your father's estate—it doesn't look good. Fortunately though, I've been approached with an offer for the house." With a somewhat scolding tone, Mr. Shepherd turned to face Walter, "When I hadn't heard a response from any of the numerous letters or phone calls regarding the terrible financial state of your affairs," Mr. Shepherd continued with a despairing look at Mr. Elliot, "I took the liberty of letting a few key individuals know, discretely of course, that you were considering selling your home if the offer was right."

Mr. Shepherd handed a paper to Elizabeth who looked it over in haste. Mr. Elliot crossed the room to view the document, and Elizabeth handed it to him. Mr. Shepherd added, "I'm pleased to tell you it's a generous offer."

"Does that mean I can keep the car after all?" inquired Mr. Elliot hopefully.

Mr. Shepherd frowned. "It's not *that* generous. Walter, you have to face facts. It took years to get this deeply in debt so it's going to take time before you're back on track. For a while, you're going to have to live on a budget. If you follow my advice, in a few years you just might end up being able to purchase quite a number of one-of-a-kind cars."

"A budget!" exclaimed Mr. Elliot in disgust. The word 'budget' was taboo to Anne's extravagant father and sister.

Mr. Shepherd didn't bother trying to hide his contempt. "Yes, join the club. Most people do live on a budget, including me. Lucky for the girls, you weren't able to touch their mother's inheritance since it's still in trust." Mr. Shepherd eyed Mr. Elliot pointedly, and their father had the decency to look shamefaced.

By now the paperwork had reached Anne. "Do we know the people who made the offer on our house?" she asked.

"I doubt it," said Mr. Shepherd. "It's a man by the name of Cedric Croft, a retired Naval Admiral. But I do recall his wife mentioning that her brother, a Mr. Wentworth, worked some odd jobs in this area some time ago."

The mention of the name "Wentworth" visibly shook Anne's countenance, and this did not go unnoticed by her sister. Ashen faced, Anne felt as if the wind had been knocked out of her. Surely it had to be Rick! Hadn't he once mentioned having an older sister whose husband was in the Navy?

Mr. Elliot's voice broke Anne's reflection. "Do you think we should accept?" Mr. Elliot asked and instantly received a nod of approval from Mr. Shepherd.

"You'd be a fool not to," he stated empathetically.

Elizabeth, who always thought ahead when it came to matters concerning herself, asked, "But where will we live?"

Mr. Shepherd assured her, "You should make enough on this offer to buy another home, though one significantly smaller."

Mr. Elliot turned to Elizabeth excitedly. "Elizabeth, remember that house we saw during our tour of the vineyards? The one where I said if I ever purchased a quaint little vacation home that would be the one?" Elizabeth nodded in remembrance. Susan, finding out they weren't totally destitute became talkative again.

"Yes, it was the one with the 'for sale' sign on it," agreed Susan.

Mr. Shepherd intervened, "Walter, if you give me sufficient information, I'll make some inquiries on your behalf."

Mr. Elliot, Elizabeth and Susan began to formulate plans for their move to California which left Anne time to ponder about the young man whose last name had just been mentioned. How could simply hearing his name have such a profound effect on her!? She tried to convince herself she was no longer the giddy, immature girl she once was—a teenager who had showed up almost daily at the country club where Rick worked. Anne blushed at remembering how she had enrolled in nearly every conceivable swim or tennis class just for the opportunity to spend time with the lifeguard who had rescued her. Over the course of that summer, a friendship had formed which progressed into something much deeper, ending in their declarations of love—at least for her. Anne now questioned the depth of Rick's feelings. Surely, his must have been nothing more than mere infatuation. *How strange fate can be. To think of Rick's sister and brother-in-law living in my house? What a funny sense of humor God has,* she ironically thought.

Chapter 4

Anne found herself upstairs with the task of cleaning out the attic. Normally this would have been a duty she dreaded, but today it provided Anne an escape from her overly stressed sister. Her father had left the two of them to pack while he attended to some business at the office—which most likely meant golfing with some old buddies of his. Despite the circumstances, Anne found herself delighting in rediscovering treasures and keepsakes passed down through her mother's side.

The Elliot's attic was like those only found in novels, holding great mysteries from the past. It had a forgotten quality about it, making one believe that hidden within were many lost secrets just waiting to be uncovered. A single window allowed a stream of natural light to reveal a dusty room overrun with boxes and vintage furniture. There was even an old dress form dating back to when her ancestors clothes were hand-made.

Reaching for a box, Anne opened the lid to find vintage *Women's Daily* magazines which most likely had belonged to her grandmother. A small cough escaped Anne from the accumulated dust. She wasn't sentimental enough to want them and knew her sisters wouldn't give them a second glance. Anne was ready to toss them in the recycle box but then changed her mind. Setting them aside, she made a mental note to see if they might sell on eBay. Considering the financial state of their family, every bit would help.

Anne then moved on to the next storage container atop a stack of old trunks against the wall. Opening it, she discovered it was her old keepsake items. Anne smiled with interest and lowered the large container to the ground, seating herself next to it. An old wooden carved box caught her eye and she pulled it out.

Inside Anne found her old report cards, a girl-scout sash and an award she'd won for the best drawing in fourth grade. She smiled at the recollection of rushing home to share the good news with her parents. The next item was Anne's acceptance into the National Honor Society. Beneath that was a book. The title read, *Persuasion* by Jane Austen.

Immediately, emotion surged inside her. The book had been a gift from Rick on her seventeenth birthday. She opened it with a sort of reverence, delicately turning its pages only to have a note slip from its hidden depths, falling to the ground. Anne's breath caught at the sight of it.

Setting the box down to reach for the letter, she unfolded it with shaking hands and looked tenderly at it. The letter showed evidence by its worn page that it had been read many times before being put to rest when she realized Rick was not returning. Viewing it once more would be painful, but she was willing to suffer the consequences. Slowly reading the discolored paper, Anne allowed Rick once again to enter her life.

My Dearest Anne,

It's almost midnight, and I can't stop thinking about you. I meant what I said tonight...I love you, and it's not just a feeling that is here today and gone tomorrow—I want to spend every moment with you forever.

Anne paused to wipe away her tears. Even now, at 25, his letter still had the power to evoke deep feelings within her. If only his words had been true.

She remembered the day he had given her this token of his love. Rick had driven her to Multnomah Falls for a picnic dinner. It was a warm summer afternoon, and just being with him made everything perfect. He had packed fried chicken, fresh fruit, and a crusty baguette, laying a soft blanket onto the plush grass.

Anne placed her hand to her cheek, remembering how he had softly caressed her face, his eyes expressing his unspoken affection. And then he said those three words...I love you. The memory brought more tears.

How can someone say and write such things, but not mean them? If they really loved you so deeply, is it possible for them to simply forget you? Yet Anne believed Rick to be sincere at the time. Despite all evidence now to the contrary, in her heart, Anne wanted to hold onto the dream that maybe he still cared, or at least once in a while thought of her with tenderness. It was the only thing that kept Anne from becoming bitter. She didn't want to think badly of him. Even after all this time, Anne held no hard feelings towards Rick. She only wished things had ended differently, but since they hadn't, Anne hoped to someday forget those memories and once again find love.

She folded the letter, but instead of returning it to the book, Anne decided to place it in the carved box alongside all the other letters Rick had given her. It was not Rick's fault his feelings had changed. Rather, it was just her misfortune that Rick had taken a huge piece of her heart which she feared she'd never get back. The thought made Anne feel so empty, and the hurt seem endless. She wished she could forget everything that had happened between them—but then another part of Anne was glad she hadn't. The happiest time in her life was when Rick loved her and they were together. But those days were long gone. Anne realized at that moment how much she had let her identity go—losing herself when Rick left. Things that had meant so much to Anne no longer brought enjoyment. Carol's words, spoken just days ago, came crashing into her thoughts, *It's time to move on and let things lie in the past.*

Perhaps Carol was right. Since Anne had not heard from Rick after all this time, she could only assume that's exactly what Rick had chosen to do. Yet the thought cut deep and the sensation left Anne feeling exposed, open for the whole world to see and pity. Yes, it was time to make herself forget.

All these years, Anne still felt emotionally tied to Rick, and never really thought of herself as being single. When others showed an interest in her, Anne discouraged them, as if somehow she would be untrue to Rick. And now, just hearing his name and coming across an old letter shook her to the core! *How pitiful is that!* If anything, it told Anne she definitely needed to take Carol's advice.

In agony, Anne wondered why she had not been able to forget him. Bowing her head, she earnestly prayed, "Dear God, please remove these feelings if they are not from you. And if Rick is not meant for me, help me to accept it."

Later, carrying a packing crate down the stairs, Anne stopped abruptly when hearing Elizabeth's voice. Peering over the railing, she spied her sister speaking on the phone.

"Yes, all the arrangements have been made, Susan. The Admiral and his wife are coming over this afternoon to look at the house before the deal is finalized. My dad's at the office, so I guess I will have to show them around."

At the mention of the Admiral and his wife, Anne nearly dropped the box she was carrying. The scuffing sound caught Elizabeth's attention, causing her to look in the direction of the stairs. Anne ducked away from sight just in time.

Elizabeth lowered her voice as a precaution, but Anne could still overhear. "I must admit, getting to meet the buyers could prove interesting. You see Anne used to date a Rick Wentworth and they got quite serious. The guy even tried to marry her! Of course, my dad didn't approve, so Rick tried to get Anne to elope with him. Fortunately, Carol was able to talk some sense into Anne and broke up their plans. I wonder if the new owners are related."

Anne slowly crept back up the stairs, carefully avoiding the step with the slightly loose board that always squeaked. Exchanging her sweatshirt for a jacket and carrying her shoes, Anne tried to walk as silently as possible to the downstairs kitchen.

Just as Anne made it to the counter to grab her keys, Elizabeth caught sight of her. "Anne! Where are you going? We're not done yet!"

"I, ahh…I'm almost out of packing tape. I was just going to get some more."

Elizabeth eyed her sister suspiciously. Luckily, Anne didn't have to lie. She was on the last roll and only had enough tape to do a few more boxes.

"Well, don't be long. Susan's coming over tonight and I want to be finished before then." Anne nodded submissively and headed out the door.

Once at Wal-Mart, with all the turmoil going on in her life, Anne's willpower flew out the door. In her cart lay not only the needed rolls of packing tape, but also two large bags of Dove chocolates. That night, she was going to drown her awakened sorrows with the goodness of two familiar and delicious friends…milk and dark chocolate.

Chapter 5

Savoring each piece of the delectable candy, Anne sat on the couch watching her favorite movie, *Sense and Sensibility*. With the exception of her own bedroom and the library, the home theater was another room Anne would greatly miss.

In this haven sat two luxurious sectional couches before a projection screen covering almost an entire wall. To complete the atmosphere, her mother installed a popcorn machine, along with a huge refrigerator cleverly designed to blend into the paneling. One could always count on finding an assortment of beverages and delicious ice cream treats housed within its doors.

Clutching a blanket, Anne viewed the point in the movie where Marianne was atop a hill looking at Willoughby's home, reciting a shared poem special to the couple. Anne mouthed the words simultaneously with Marianne, sharing equally in the pain. She both loved and hated this scene, as it always made Anne recall the depth of her own feelings for Rick, and the remorse she still carried within.

As such, Anne felt a deep affinity with this heroine's character, even in temperament and enthusiasm for life. Like Marianne, Anne had to watch the vitality she once possessed be zapped from her by the loss of Rick's love. Although Rick was a man of character, whereas Willoughby was not, Anne could still identify with the unparalleled oneness that set Willoughby and Marianne apart from other relationships. Anne pondered how losing one's first love affects a woman—it alters the way she carries herself, her thoughts about romance, and even the way she interacts with others. There's a hidden sadness behind a woman's eyes that never leaves, only slightly fading with the prospect of a new love. Affairs of the heart indelibly have the power to define and shape a woman.

The shrill sound of a phone spoiled this sob-worthy moment. With mild irritation, Anne wondered if anyone would answer it. To her relief the ringing stopped. Satisfied, Anne popped another dark chocolate in her mouth only to see Elizabeth enter the room while speaking on the phone.

"Of course Anne can go…"

At hearing her name, Anne looked over questioningly. Elizabeth, seeing loose candy wrappers all around, sent her sibling a critical look. Anne quickly pushed the remaining evidence of the yet uneaten chocolates behind her back to avoid confiscation.

Elizabeth lowered the phone to speak, "Anne, Mary's sick and needs help with the boys. We're all done here, so that means you're not needed anymore."

Elizabeth's last statement made Anne feel about as valuable as one of the empty candy wrappers lying beside her. Anne clearly wasn't important to Elizabeth. In fact, it was hard to believe they were even sisters. After her mother died, Anne felt as if she didn't have a family, at least not one that made her feel cared about as a person. Sure, her other sister Mary 'needed' her, but Anne knew it was only because Mary wanted a resident cook, bottle washer and babysitter.

Mary, being the youngest, was used to getting her way, having been catered to excessively. To make matters worse, after losing their mother at only eleven, Mary became the prime candidate for doting old ladies and a widowed father who constantly showered her with every whim.

However, the opportunity to escape the stress of losing their home was inviting to Anne. She shrugged and nodded in agreement.

Elizabeth put the phone back up to her mouth and turned to leave. "Yes, she'll come tomorrow. Okay, love you too, Sis, goodbye."

Chapter 6

Anne wanted sympathy. She decided to call Carol.

"How long will you be gone?" asked the empathetic voice over the phone.

Turning out the lights and climbing into bed, Anne shrugged. "A few weeks…"

"Have you thought about what you'll do once you're done at Mary's?" inquired Carol.

"I guess I'll move to California for the time being. Dad wants me to go check out the new house. You'll come and see it too, won't you?" asked Anne as she plumped her pillow and repositioned herself beneath the sheets.

"Yes, I'd love to. What about your work?"

Anne hesitated, "I don't know yet. I'll finish up those designs I've been working on and send them to you next week." Anne realized life was going to change rapidly for her in more ways than just business deadlines…would she be ready?

Early the next morning, packing the last item she planned to take to Mary's, Anne glanced around her now barren room. It was weird to think that her home, the only one she had ever known, would no longer belong to her anymore. Anne was going to miss it, even more so because of her mother. She decided to give the house one final walk-through before heading to Mary's.

As she toured the home, Anne couldn't help but admire how grand it was. The Elliot estate boasted twelve large bedrooms (not including the old servant's quarters), each of which had their own walk-in closet and bathroom. There were two kitchens, a large study, a craft room, two dining rooms, an indoor and outdoor dinette, an in-home theatre, two family rooms, a grand living room, a dance floor, workout room, and an outdoor swimming pool and tennis court. The location of the home was ideal—just twenty-five minutes from downtown Portland, yet situated in the quiet and secluded West Hills—making it a realtor's dream sale.

The first room Anne meandered through was her father's study. It was spacious with dark mahogany paneling and provided a beautiful view overlooking the well-kept backyard garden. One normally associated a study with lots of books, but Mr. Elliot's den was the exception. A built-in flat screen television hung on the wall and reminded Anne more of a sport's haven—her father watched football and baseball religiously. She would miss seeing him there cheering on his beloved Jets and Yankees.

Next, Anne wandered down the long hall into the home's craft room. This had been her mother's favorite place in the house. Mrs. Elliot had loved scrap-booking so the room was always well stocked with supplies. Anne had come in a few times after her mother's passing, attempting to put together a few pages of memories—but it just seemed so empty without her mother there. The large window housed inside caught Anne's attention. It was a beautiful day, and it granted a picturesque view of the pool. Anne smiled. She had spent many hours out in that pool with her sisters. The three of them had much fun playing Marco Polo, making up synchronized swimming routines, and giving each other scores on their fantasy Olympic diving competitions. That was when Anne and her sisters were more like friends, not just siblings.

Too bad things change. Anne wished she and her sisters were closer, but since high school they all seemed to go in separate ways. For Elizabeth, the change came after discovering she was considered a beauty. From that point on, Elizabeth only worked on her appearance, failing to develop her personality or put much emphasis on family relationships. It made Anne sad just thinking about it. To compound things, Anne had lived on campus at Willamette University and Mary had gotten married after turning eighteen. Anne mused at how different three people could be when they each shared the same two parents. She had hoped that when she moved back home from college things would be different between herself and Elizabeth, but it was in vain. Anne sensed that her eldest sister only suffered her company because she was useful and could be trusted. Elizabeth didn't particularly care for Anne, and Carol thought it stemmed from jealousy. Anne was loved and appreciated by all, whereas Elizabeth was not.

Anne stood outside the master bedroom, looking at the large, plushly-made four-poster bed. Since the new house was smaller, her father agreed to sell a number of furnishings to the new owners—this bed was one of them. Anne remembered the times when an occasional nightmare had awakened her, and how she'd run downstairs, seeking safety and finding it as she crawled into the arms of her parents. Anne had to confess that on some occasions, even though she wasn't scared, she'd still use that as an excuse to snuggle between the two of them in bed. Oh, how she missed those days…and how much she would miss this house!

Chapter 7

Visiting Mary was not one of Anne's favorite things to do. She loved her sister, but simply put—Mary's world revolved around Mary. Her sister had no problem voicing her 'sorrows' to anyone who would listen and as a result, it dragged Anne down emotionally. Mary imagined herself frequently sick, most of the time in order to obtain attention and sympathy—two things Mary loved getting. Anne couldn't understand how her sister's husband, Charles, could put up with it. But then, how did Anne? The answer: they both loved Mary. Charles was exceptionally patient and although their matrimonial relationship wasn't perfect, he usually had a way of coping with Mary's episodes.

In looks, Mary didn't really favor any of the Elliot's. Instead, she was more of a mixture of her parents, therefore creating her own unique look. Mary kept her hair curly and highlighted, suiting her round and cheerful-looking face. She was the shortest of all three girls, and had a cute figure despite being the only one of the siblings who had given birth, twice in fact. Anne adored her nephews.

Dreading her sister's antics, Anne chose to take the long way to Mary's. By taking the back roads, it increased the commute by at least an hour and Anne relished the idea of having some quiet time to herself. It was a beautiful, sunny day, yet a little too hot for Anne's liking. Clear skies and a high of 85 degrees was what the weatherman had predicted—but upon opening her window, Anne thought surely he must be off by about ten degrees. After experiencing the super heated blast of air, it quickly prompted the 'no open windows' enactment and the A/C policy was strictly enforced.

As Anne drove along the country roads in her cute little Honda Fit, she sang out loud with the radio blaring. The accompanying road noise helped to drown out any imperfections, making Anne believe she might be a close second to Mariah Carey. Who says you can only sound good in the shower? While Anne exercised her vocal chords, her eyes feasted on the endearing scenery of long established family farms, antique homes with lovely gardens, and unending fields of local crops.

She pushed the radio button to change the station when all of the sudden Anne heard several thumps as well as noticing a lack of control in steering. Instinctively, she slowed down and looked through the rear-view and side mirrors. The latter showed what Anne suspected—a flat tire. She pulled over and got outside the car to survey the extent of damage.

Anne bent over to look closer at the deflated tire. To her dismay, she spotted a nail piercing the tread. Sighing, she headed back to the driver's seat to grab her cell phone. No signal! The back roads may be beautiful, but all of the sudden, Anne felt quite isolated with no way of reaching civilization. Rolling her eyes, she trudged back to the trunk of the car to open it. How was she supposed to change this tire?! Anne had never changed one in her life. The only person she'd ever seen do this was Rick. She could still remember the event vividly.

The two were coming back from visiting his older brother, Ethan, who pastored a church near the outskirts of town. They had attended the evening service, followed by tea and dessert at the parsonage. Pastor Wentworth was a slightly older, less athletic version of Rick who served the best carrot cake Anne had ever tasted. She had adored Ethan and the way he had made her feel so welcomed. She enjoyed her time there so much that she was sad to leave. Listening to Rick and his brother swap old stories and memories seemed ideal, so it was with regret Anne and Rick finally left to make the three hour drive back to Portland. Just an hour into the return trip, Anne had heard thumps similar to the ones experienced today, and panicked. Rick pulled over and soothingly assured her everything would be all right. Instead of getting impatient or upset about the inconvenience, Rick ended up turning the situation into something fun while he changed the tire. Before Anne knew it, they were back on the road, leaving her wishing it had taken longer. But that was just like Rick; he had the ability to turn a mishap into an adventure. If only she had someone to make her laugh now. All Anne wanted to do at that moment was sit on the bumper and have a good cry, but she refused to give up so easily.

Taking the jack and lug wrench out of the trunk, Anne set them beside the busted tire. Now what? How was it that Rick used this thingy to hoist up the car? Anne grunted as she struggled with no success to budge the fastened nuts, and after a few minutes finally took a rest. Anne wished she'd paid more attention back then. Instead, she'd spent most of the time admiring Rick's muscular frame, and who could blame her? He had looked so manly as he made the repair. Trying once again, Anne made a few more half-hearted attempts before signaling her surrender by throwing the 'useless' tools back into the car, exchanging them for her luggage. Taking another deep breath, Anne started her trek down the road.

Twenty minutes later, Anne was sweating like a pig. She struggled with the bags, and her shoulders and arms were aching from their weight. It seemed as if she'd walked nearly fifty miles in the searing sun, but realistically it was probably closer to two. At finally spotting civilization ahead, a flood of relief overcame her. Anne recognized Uppercross Street and mustered her remaining willpower to continue, knowing she was almost there. Normally Anne enjoyed the fact that Mary lived on an incline, as it offered a beautiful view. But being hot, tired, and carrying difficult luggage, she now wished for flatter terrain. The sight of her sister's estate had never been so inviting as it was now with its promise of a refreshing shower, shade, and a glass of ice cold water.

Mary's place was big, with lots of strategically placed windows to catch the ever-constant sun. Her sister had decorated the entire house with a patriotic theme. The home was charming. Adding to its appeal was the wrap-around porch and a small wooden swing. It also boasted a volleyball and basketball court in the backyard, which sadly was hardly used.

When she reached the front door to ring the bell, Anne let the luggage fall in a heap at her ankles.

"Anne!" Mary scolded with irritation upon answering the door. "What took you so long?" Mary looked beyond Anne to the empty driveway. "Where's your car?" Anne pretended to ignore her sister's upset manner and entered the house. As she did so, Mary got a whiff of her sibling and flinched, waving a hand to deflect the sweat-drenched odor Anne was emitting. "Oh, my goodness, you smell terrible!"

Anne blushed. "Believe me, if I had known that I'd end up walking several miles in this heat, I would have put on extra deodorant."

Mary grimaced, "You do realize that the kids have been pestering me like crazy wondering when you'd arrive?!"

"Sorry," Anne explained, "It wasn't intentional. I got a flat tire."

Unimpressed, Mary answered, "Well, the timing couldn't have been worse! Here I am, not feeling at all well and then this happens! Why couldn't you have left earlier? Instead of me being able to rest in bed, I've been up with the children all this time. I am always so tired, I only wish people could be more considerate! The doctors don't even know what's wrong with me!"

Before Mary could go on with her complaints, Nicholas and Little Charlie ran to bombard their favorite aunt with hugs. This welcome pleased Anne as she looked tenderly into their beaming faces.

The boys were a year and a half apart. Nicholas was the eldest with sandy blonde hair and cute dimples just like his father. Anne was certain that he'd be quite the heartbreaker when he grew up. Little Charlie was already taller than his older brother. He favored Mary's looks and had dark brown hair like his mother, even though currently Mary's tresses were bleached a fashionable blonde. Little Charlie had a smile that could melt even the coldest heart.

"Aunt Anne! Will you play with us?" their voices rang out in unison.

Anne lowered herself to her knees. "Of course! What do you want to play?"

"Mom just taught us Rock, Paper, Scissors. Do you know how to play that?" asked Little Charlie.

This bit of information was refreshing. *At least my sister's been spending time with them now,* thought Anne. She demonstrated her best Rock, Paper, Scissor skills for the boys who laughed.

Mary began to usher the boys away. "Okay, time to leave Aunt Anne alone." Mary grabbed the trays that held the remains of the kids' afternoon snacks. There was one Twinkie left. As she headed for the kitchen, Mary unwrapped it.

Over her shoulder she said to Anne, "Hurry up and take a shower, Sis, we're expected at my in-laws in an hour." Anne nodded and began picking up her bags.

Mary returned tray-free and with a half-eaten Twinkie in hand. "I'm not looking forward to tonight though. It wouldn't be so bad if Clara would stop giving the boys candy. After Grandma has them sufficiently wound up on a sugar-high, guess who gets to take them home?...ME! I try so hard to only feed the boys healthy snacks."

Anne looked with raised eyebrows at the Twinkie. "Where's Charles?" she asked instead, changing the subject.

"Hunting...where else?" Mary replied with disgust. "You know, Anne, I think Charles does it to provoke me." Mary inhaled the last bite of Twinkie, continuing to talk with her mouth full, "But the one thing you can count on is that he'll be home in time for dinner. All he thinks about is hunting and food! But me, I hardly have an appetite these days, what with me feeling so ill." Anne smiled at Mary's exasperated expression and *very* healthy appetite.

Chapter 8

Mary's in-laws, Stanley and Clara Musgrove, were the kindest and most welcoming couple. There was no lack of love or warmth in their company, and that trait extended to their children. Charles was the oldest followed by Louise and Etta. Both girls were now out of high school. Louise was almost twenty-one and Etta, nineteen.

When Mary, Anne and the boys arrived at the Musgrove's that evening, they let themselves in the front door. They were greeted by laughter and voices coming from the den.

"We're in here!" Clara yelled.

Following Mary into the den, Anne walked in holding the hands of her nephews to find the family enjoying a round of cards.

The Musgrove's home looked like something out of *Better Homes and Gardens*. The style was simple but elegant, and flowers were always in season. Mrs. Musgrove had a very green thumb.

"Anne!" Louise and Etta cried out with excitement.

At spotting their grandpa, Little Charlie and Nicholas ran to him for a hug before quickly turning to their grandma who was always ready to embrace them. She whispered to the boys, "Come quickly into the kitchen; I just baked snickerdoodles!"

Clara was a heavyset woman, but the extra padding suited her. She had a youthfulness about her despite her age, and was always ready to be of help. She had the biggest heart of anybody Anne knew.

As Clara returned from her errand of treating the boys, she exclaimed, "Oh, Anne! We're so glad you're here! The girls were so excited to hear you were coming."

"Anne, come and sit," Mr. Musgrove said as he patted the seat nearest himself and his wife.

Anne glanced at Mary who looked slightly miffed at the attention Anne was receiving. Mrs. Musgrove noticed the exchange. "You too, Mary," she added diplomatically.

"How was your drive?" Louise eagerly asked Anne.

Anne grimaced. "Wonderful, until I got a flat tire and had to walk a couple of miles with my luggage in tow."

"Yes, and she smelled something awful," Mary quickly interjected. The snide comment caused a momentary silence after this disclosure. Anne blushed profusely, wondering why her sister always seemed to go out of her way to embarrass her.

Thankfully, Stanley was a jolly, pleasant man with a good sense of humor. Although youthful in heart like his beloved Clara, his face showed his maturity. He spent many an hour outdoors on the lake fishing or tending his gardens.

"Well…" he said as he deliberately inhaled the air near Anne. "I'm pleased to report the coast is clear! She seems to have fully recovered."

Everyone was glad for an excuse to finally laugh, having the awkward moment now behind them. Anne smiled brightly and was glad to be able to chuckle at herself as well.

"Where does your family plan to settle, now that your place has been sold?" Mrs. Musgrove asked Anne later as they chopped vegetables for dinner.

"My dad has purchased a house in Napa Valley, California. He and Elizabeth spotted it on one of their trips," Anne explained.

Louise wandered into the kitchen and overheard Anne's remark. "I hope we get to go to California this summer. It would be great to visit Anne," Louise said, grabbing a carrot to munch on. Anne brightened at the suggestion and indeed hoped it would come to pass.

Louise could be summed up in one word: Fun. She was cute, spunky, entertaining...you name it. She loved the outdoors, and her skin's beautiful golden glow reflected it. Her hair was thick, curly and brown with natural deep red highlights. She usually pulled half of it up or just let it hang down below her shoulder blades.

Louise reached for another veggie, offering one to Anne. "No more or you'll spoil your appetite," chided Mrs. Musgrove.

Louise paused in her chewing to give Anne a puzzled look, then holding up the celery stick for all to see, both girls burst into laughter.

Mrs. Musgrove chuckled, realizing how odd her comment must have sounded after considering what Louise was eating. To save face, Clara declared, "Alright, you got me on that, but it's also said, 'He who shall not work shall not eat'. So either start chopping or remove yourself. I'll have no scavengers in my kitchen."

"Okay! I'm going." Louise shoved the remaining bite into her mouth and then spanked her mother playfully before leaving.

"Incorrigible brat!" Mrs. Musgrove chuckled. Then with a smile she added, "I'll call you when dinner's ready."

Mrs. Musgrove went to the sink to rinse her hands, then grabbed a handful of veggies to place them into a pan. "You have a way with people, Anne," said Mrs. Musgrove. Anne smiled as Clara continued, "...especially with the children. I haven't seen them this well behaved since, well, since you were last here."

Anne looked surprised, "But that was last summer!"

Mrs. Musgrove reached for additional veggies and checked to see if Mary was nearby and thus might overhear. "You'd think as a grandmother I'd wish to have the children over more, but the way they're being raised...so rambunctious and unsupervised." Anne lowered her head, embarrassed for her sister's sake. Mrs. Musgrove grabbed the last few celery and carrot bits and began seasoning the dish. "I don't think your sister likes to bring them over here much, either. She says I give them too many sweets." Anne had to smile at hearing that, remembering her sister's earlier comment. "Well, honestly, Anne, how am I supposed to get them to behave if I don't have a few bribes up my sleeves? Let's be realistic, vegetables just don't do the trick. Besides, the boys are skinny as it is."

Anne laughed. No matter how blunt or opinionated Mrs. Musgrove was, she loved her for it.

Chapter 9

The party sat salivating at the table with grumbling stomachs as the aroma of a promised dinner escaped from the kitchen. They had waited as long as they could for Charles to arrive but fearing the dinner would soon become ruined, the family decided to begin without him.

Mrs. Musgrove brought out a steaming plate of pot roast to the sounds of "oohs" and "awes". The array of tender potatoes, carrots and celery, and moist beef lay nicely displayed on the beautiful silver serving dish.

"It looks wonderful!" Etta said.

After placing the delicious looking food on the table, Mrs. Musgrove sat and laid her napkin on her lap, then looked towards her husband. "Honey, will you say the blessing?"

Stanley Musgrove nodded and they bowed their heads and prayed over the food, remembering to bless the hands that prepared it. In unison, the group said 'Amen' and began passing the food around the table.

"We always love it when guests come. That's about the only time Clara cooks a feast these days," Stanley complained. The group laughed at this announcement as Mrs. Musgrove blushed and came to her own defense.

"I admit it!" Then glancing at her daughters she continued, "But it's only because my girls are so picky. I've just given up." There was more laughter to be heard as Louise and Etta agreed with their mother.

The sound of the front door being opened interrupted their laughter. "It must be Charles!" exclaimed Mrs. Musgrove in anticipation. She turned in the direction of the entrance and shouted, "We're in the dining room!"

Charles entered and saw the open seat next to Mary, but his wife's face held an unwelcome expression due to him being over an hour late. He came up beside Mary to kiss the side of her head, but she pulled away. The rest of the family looked down in embarrassment at witnessing this, and sheepishly Charles proceeded to sit.

Anne's brother-in-law was a nice-looking man of average height. He had that sportsman look about him and always appeared to have a five o'clock shadow that covered his strong jaw and upper lip. He was kind and outgoing, the type of friend one could count on to be there in a crisis. Anne loved Charles like a real brother.

"It's good to see you, Anne," he said, recovering.

"You too, Charles," she replied.

Mrs. Musgrove began piling food onto her son's plate. "Sorry, we couldn't wait any longer. Your dad's stomach was speaking full sentences!"

"How was hunting today?" Mr. Musgrove asked.

Charles looked bummed. "Didn't get a stinking thing."

"Nothing?" Clara asked with surprise.

"My Chuck said he didn't have any luck either," Etta commented.

Etta was the quieter of the two Musgrove girls, though still quite outgoing. She possessed an untouched sweetness about her and a lively glow to her cheeks which was nicely framed by her cute bobbed golden brown hair. At times, Etta was known to be rather indecisive and relied heavily on Louise to help her make decisions. Now having a steady beau, Etta liked to update everyone on *her* Chuck and to express his many opinions on subjects. Her brother Charles acknowledged Etta's comment with an explanation.

"It's all due to that development on the other side of the hill. It's scaring away the game," Charles said with a hint of frustration.

"What type of development?" Anne asked.

"Residential contractors are getting hungry for land. They've used up all the flat plains on the west side and are now moving into the hills." Charles said, perturbed.

"That's too bad," Anne said.

"You're telling me!" Charles responded. "Pretty soon there'll be no wilderness left." Charles took a mouthful of beef and then looked sweetly at his unhappy Mary, hoping a tender look might change her irritable, foul mood, but to no avail.

Not long after dinner, Mary chose to take the boys home early in her car so she could put them to bed. This left Anne to drive back with Charles in his Subaru Outback. The two had known each other for years, and they talked like old friends. Anne was the type of person whom people could easily confide in and share their thoughts. Now being 'brother' and 'sister', their bond had grown even closer.

"How's life treating you? Is your card business going well?" Charles asked as he adjusted his seatbelt.

"Yes, very well. In fact, Hallmark is even considering giving me my own signature line."

Charles smiled with genuine happiness. "Anne, that's wonderful!"

Pleased, Anne responded, "Thanks...and how about you?"

"Fine. Business is booming actually." Anne could tell by his tone however that something was bothering him. It was confirmed when he looked over at her with a more serious face. "If only a family could be as easy as business...but you probably didn't need to be told that. You saw your sister tonight...she thinks I don't help with the children. And when I do, Mary says I spoil the boys. I could manage them very well if it were not for her interference. And lately, Mary's complaining about being ill all the time, but so far, the only thing I see that makes her truly sick is me." He looked at Anne and noticed her discomfort. "I'm sorry. I didn't mean to burden you with this, but you've always been so easy to talk with. It seems everything gets better somehow when you're here..." Charles paused, looking gratefully at Anne. "I'm glad you've come, Sis."

Later that night, while brushing her teeth, Anne couldn't help but overhear an argument between Charles and Mary.

"...how would you know, you're never here!" yelled Mary in accusation.

"Maybe I'd be home more if I'd find a clean house and a happy wife waiting for me," Charles retorted.

"Unbelievable!" Mary shrieked, "You just don't get it, do you?! How is that supposed to happen when I never get any help!" Immediately afterwards, a door could be heard slamming.

A few minutes later, Anne heard a knock. She quickly spit out the toothpaste and paused. Soon realizing it was not the bathroom door, but instead the one recently slammed, she relaxed. Anne heard Charles say contritely, "I'm sorry, Mary. Please open up."

Anne's heart was softened by the hurt sound in Charles' voice, thinking her sister would surely succumb to his plea. However, only silence ensued and eventually Anne heard dejected footsteps pad softly down the hallway. Once Anne finished her toiletries and was certain the coast was clear, she quietly exited the bathroom. Sleepy after her tiring day, Anne got into bed, sitting there for a moment before leaning over to turn off the nightstand lamp. A knock at the door startled her.

"Aunt Anne?" Anne heard Nicholas' frightened voice through the door.

"Come in," she responded. Nicholas slowly turned the knob and entered. "Is everything okay?" Anne asked, melting at the sight of her small nephew in his oversized night-shirt.

"Can I sleep with you?" Nicholas whispered. "I'm scared."

"But what about your mommy and daddy?" She knew her sister would be hurt if she found out Nicholas had come to her instead of his mother.

"Mommy doesn't let me sleep with her." The quiver in Nicholas' voice caused Anne's heart to break a thousand times over. She patted the bed and Nicholas came leaping in. Helping him under the covers, Anne allowed him to cuddle up next to her.

Wrapping her arms around him and kissing the back of his head, she stared at the ceiling, engrossed in thought. *Poor baby. Does my sister know what she is doing to this family?*

Chapter 10

Anne awakened the next morning to discover the sun streaming through her bedroom window and the green grassy meadows beckoning her. She glanced over at her nephew to find him still in a deep sleep. His sweet, innocent face brought a smile to her lips, and she hoped that someday, God willing, she'd have children of her own. She softly stroked his hair, and was tempted to stay in bed all morning but realized she must get up, as she knew a big day ahead of her. Anne had promised the boys an adventure, and their aunt always kept her word.

Packing a lunch for her nephews was a no-brainer: string cheese, a big bag of Cheetos, plus peanut butter and jelly sandwiches with the crusts cut off. With that task accomplished, Anne was ready to take on the world, or at least a few insects or any reptiles they might encounter along the way. The trio left in high spirits with an agenda to have fun, taking their bikes to explore the surrounding woods. Two enjoyable hours later, the threesome found themselves with satisfied tummies, dirt-stained knees and full of giggles.

Leaving their bikes temporarily behind, they strolled through a meadow of yard-stick high grass, their wild imaginations beginning to transport them from the countryside to a land far away. In this adventure, the threesome believed themselves to be famous explorers on a scientific venture, classifying rare insects and animal life.

"What do you think we should call him, Aunt Anne?" Little Charlie asked, holding a green amphibian in his hand.

Anne studied the wild bull frog she and Little Charlie had captured. The boys were terribly excited with this new find and were determined the frog was to be their new pet.

"What about the name Freddie?" Anne suggested.

Little Charlie laughed, "No! That's a dumb name. How about Superman?" Now it was Anne's turn to laugh.

"Look! There's Grandpa," Nicholas said, prompting Little Charlie and Anne's immediate attention. "But who's that with him?" he asked inquisitively.

Anne squinted to get a better look. Her eyesight couldn't quite compete with that of her young nephews, but there was something about the man—his walk and mannerism seemed to strike a chord deep within her—yet Anne couldn't make sense of it. As she continued to observe the stranger engaged in conversation with Mr. Musgrove, she began to feel faint as her heartbeat accelerated. Dropping instantly to her knees, she took shelter within the tall grass.

"What's wrong, Aunt Anne?" Little Charlie asked with concern.

Nicholas chimed in, "Are you okay?"

With a shaky voice, Anne answered, "I, ahhh, I'm not sure..." Maintaining her surveillance of the men through the dense grass, she found herself overwhelmed by a sudden, unexplainable anxiety attack.

"Should I go get Grandpa?" Little Charlie asked Nicholas who nodded his agreement.

Seized with fear, Anne exclaimed, "No!" and grasped Little Charlie's arm to keep him from moving. The last thing she wanted was her nephews calling attention to Mr. Musgrove and the stranger. "Umm..." Anne stalled, quickly trying to strategize all routes of escape, "Ahhh...your Aunt Anne isn't feeling very well and needs to go home right away."

Nicholas and Little Charlie exchanged confused glances, mingled with disappointment at having their fun cut short.

Anne swiftly scrambled to formulate how she could turn a quick 'get-away' into a fun game the boys would buy into.

With a disgruntled look, Little Charlie started to stand upright, but was quickly jerked down to a prone position by his panicked aunt.

"Listen up, guys," she said in a conspiratorial voice, "We need to go home in a very special way," and then, using her best 'secret agent' look, Anne finally managed to secure her nephews undivided attention. She followed this line of intrigue by asking them to recall a show they had viewed the night before. "Remember watching *Star Wars: The Clone Wars*, and how Anakin and Ahoska had to hide from General Grievous and make their way back to their space shuttle?" The boys nodded eagerly. "Well, that's exactly what we're going to pretend to do. This means we have to be really, really sneaky and quiet."

"But who will be General Grievous?" Nicholas asked, threatening to be difficult.

"Your grandpa, of course," Anne answered, and not waiting for Nick's reply, she took his hand and began showing the boys the art of squat-walking backwards through the tall grass while maintaining eye contact on the men. "If you see them look over this way, we must all fall flat on our backs as to avoid detection, okay?" The boys nodded, but each had further questions.

"Where's our space shuttle?" demanded Little Charlie.

Taken off guard and ill-prepared to answer, Anne paused for a mere second before inspiration hit. "Our bikes, of course!" When the boys looked unconvinced, Anne continued, "They're like our space...ahhh...bike pods..."

Nicholas sighed, exasperated. "They're called *speeder* bikes."

Anne nodded, "Oh yes, that's what I meant. Our bikes are speeder bikes."

"That's corny!" Nicholas snorted.

"Come on, guys!" Anne was nearing the end of her rope. "Use your imagination!"

The boys became somewhat mollified, but Little Charlie hadn't fully bought in, asking Anne one question she had hoped to avoid, "Then who's that with General Grievous?" he asked.

"How about Cad Bane?" Nicholas answered with a grin, finally getting into it.

"Can I be Anakin?" Little Charlie asked Anne, already knowing what his older brother's answer would be.

"I'm Anakin," Nicholas flatly stated.

"But you're always Anakin," Little Charlie complained.

Cutting off Nicholas' reply, Anne decided to nip this argument in the bud before it got out of hand. "Boys!" she called their attention with a hushed whisper. "If you aren't quiet, General Grievous is going to catch us!"

The boys immediately got into character, scoping the field for any sign of General Grievous' robotic army.

With this momentary success, Anne continued, "Nicholas, you be Obi-Wan, the more *experienced, wise* one, I'll be Ahoska, and Little Charlie will be Anakin, okay?" She dared to hope that Nicholas would be swayed by hearing the strong attributes of Obi-Wan, but she was unfortunately mistaken.

"But Obi-Wan wasn't in that episode," Nicholas contradicted.

"Well, we can make him be in the episode Nicholas, this is our make believe," Anne reasoned.

It only took Nicholas a minute to accept. "Okay, we'll make our own adventure then," Nicholas announced with excited eyes. "I'll be Obi-Wan, Little Charlie is Anakin, and Aunt Anne is Ahoska."

Little Charlie was stunned at first, dumbfounded that he'd actually gotten his way. When the force of it hit him, he quickly started putting in his two-bits on how the show should be run, and Anne realized she was about to lose control of the game she had created.

"Is that a light-saber sound I hear?" Anne tried once again to distract them. "We've got to move out quickly!" she whispered, pretending to get into it. The boys, now being motivated to move swiftly, each crab-walked backwards towards the cloaking shelter of the woods where their bikes awaited them. All the while, Anne had to keep reminding her nephews to cease their incessant chatter or else it might ruin their escape.

Thankfully, the boys played out their roles wonderfully, and despite the bickering between "Obi-Wan" and his "young Padawan", Anne, aka "Ahoska", was able to assist them in making it back to their "speeder bikes" without mishap. So, minus a few scrapes and nicks each received on their hands, they completed their escape quite successfully, much to the pleasure of the boys.

Once safely back at her sister's home, Anne immediately went to her room and closed the door behind her, pausing to regain her composure. Gathering up her courage, Anne walked with unsteady legs towards the bedroom dresser to open a drawer. Inside, she reached for a jewelry bag and dumped the contents out onto her bed. With trembling fingers, Anne quickly pawed through all the trinkets until at last she saw it. With hands that still shook, Anne singled out the specific item she had been looking for…a heart-shaped locket.

Grasping the necklace, Anne remembered the occasion when Rick had given it to her. It was summer, and Anne surprised Rick by taking him to the Oregon State Fair for his birthday. He had never been to a fair before. They spent the day enjoying some hair-raising rides, played a few games of chance, and finally found themselves taking in the evening's featured musical performance. It was there that Rick surprised Anne. Under the stars, while listening to an unknown country singer on stage, he gave her this delicate gift. Anne had been so touched to think that on "his" day, Rick instead thought of her. She treasured it then, and if truth be told, it was still one of her most precious items.

Opening the locket with unsteady hands, Anne knew the memories which she had strived so hard to suppress could not be wrong. Despite all logic telling her it could not be so, her heart was telling her different. Although it had been over seven years, her inner being knew no one but Rick could ever evoke such strong emotions in her like she experienced today out in the meadow. Staring down at the picture of her beloved, she knew without a doubt that the stranger talking with Mr. Musgrove and the young man in the picture encased in her heart-shaped locket were one in the same.

"Anne, are you in there?" Mary asked through the door.

Anne jumped at hearing her sister's voice. She quickly closed the locket and composed herself, concealing it tightly in her grasp. "Ahh…yes, come in."

Mary entered. "Are you okay? The boys said you were acting a little weird."

Anne peered outside her room into the hallway at the boys, looking at them as if to say, *Thanks for giving your aunt away!* "Yes, I was just feeling a little faint. Probably too much sun," she said to Mary, who seemed satisfied with her answer.

"Good. I was hoping we wouldn't have to cancel for tonight."

"Tonight? What's going on?"

"Oh, Charles' mom called while you and the boys were out. Seems a renter from one of those huge vacation homes came over today and introduced himself. Apparently he's single, so that was enough to secure him an invitation to dinner." Mary laughed at her own comment.

Anne's thoughts raced… *Was the renter Rick? He's still single?!?*

Mary continued, "Clara is such a matchmaker! I swear, my mother-in-law won't be happy until both of her daughters are married. Dinner's at seven-thirty, but Clara wants us to arrive at seven. Heaven knows why we're eating so late."

Anne mustered up the courage to ask, "Did she happen to mention the man's name?" Anne could barely hear herself speak over the beating of her own heart.

Mary spotted Anne's card designs lying on her bedside table and started flipping through them as she replied, "Yes. It's some guy named Rick Wentworth." Anne's head jerked up at hearing his name. "Must be a coincidence, huh?" Mary said, looking up at Anne. "Hey, these are really good, Sis. I'm impressed."

Normally, Anne would have loved this unexpected and rare praise from her sister, but instead she was keen to return Mary to the previous subject. "Thank you, but, you were saying about this coincidence…"

Mary glanced Anne's way. "Oh…when I first heard the name Wentworth, I thought it might be that guy you used to date but quickly dismissed that idea." Mary chuckled. "There's no way he could afford to rent one of those trendy vacation houses. I hear they're at least $5,000 a week!"

Perplexed, Anne gazed down at the locket still clasped tightly in her hand.

Chapter 11

Anne was a wreck trying to prepare herself for that evening. Since Mary was convinced the man was not Anne's former boyfriend, Anne did nothing to dissuade her sister differently. After all, the evening ahead would reveal the truth. Still, Anne was puzzled. Why was Rick spending time with the Musgroves, and how was it that he had that type of money to pay such an exorbitant rent? But Anne knew she needed to concentrate on more important things, like what she was going to wear!

After looking through every piece of clothing she had brought, Anne then invaded Mary's closet, hoping to find the perfect outfit in which to greet an old flame. But she was out of luck. Even in her wildest dreams, Anne never expected to run into Rick this weekend, and therefore had not packed with this in mind. Instead, Anne brought mostly casual basics, and only threw in two dresses just in case they went out. Her first ensemble made her look like she'd put on a few pounds. She probably had, but she didn't want to advertise it. Her only evening dress was too fancy, prompting Anne to wonder at the reaction if she showed up in that. No way did she want to look desperate! Anne finally settled on an outfit that would suffice, using a basic black skirt and a dressier top but made a mental note to go on an emergency shopping spree just in case another encounter with Rick occurred.

At five o'clock, Anne's hair was done and she was putting on the final touches of lipstick when she heard Mary yelling hysterically. Anne rushed from the bathroom to see Mary standing at the front door crying frantically.

"What's wrong!?!" Anne asked.

With terror in her eyes, Mary gasped, "Its Nicholas. He's fallen from a tree! Oh, Anne!" Mary let out a sob, "He's unconscious!"

Instantly, Anne took charge. "Did you move him?"

Mary shook her head, now overcome with grief and unable to speak. Anne looked beyond Mary to the yard outside to see Little Charlie kneeling next to his motionless brother under a large tree.

"Okay," Anne said calmly, "You need to stay with Nicholas while I call an ambulance."

Mary nodded and turned to head back to her sons.

"Mary!" Anne yelled, catching her sister. "Do you know where Charles is?"

Mary shook her head while wiping away spilling tears. Anne immediately headed for the phone. As she dialed 9-1-1, Anne prayed for Nicholas, hoping to still the anxiety she was feeling. "Dear God. Please, please let him be alright."

The operator picked up, "Black Butte 9-1-1, what's your emergency?"

Bracing herself to stay calm Anne began, "There's been an accident..."

Chapter 12

A few hours later, after safely arriving at the hospital, Nicholas was sitting in bed eating his dinner while sipping some apple juice and watching cartoons. Little Charlie sat silently on the empty bed next to him, enjoying the crayons and coloring book the nurse had brought in earlier. Now that Nicholas was alert and conscious, Mary was back to herself again, looking tired and bored. Her comments mostly consisted of complaints surrounding how she abhorred the way hospitals smelled or how bad the food tasted. Anne watched the boys from the end of Nicholas' bed, glad that Nick was okay. She offered up a silent praise to God for Nicholas' stable condition. It had been a miracle her nephew hadn't been seriously injured.

Hurried footsteps echoed in the hall outside. In a panicked state Charles rushed in, and with a strained voice croaked, "What happened?" He was greeted with smiles from all, and the tension in his face evaporated at the sight of Nicholas sitting cheerfully in bed.

"Charles!" "Daddy!" chimed Mary and Little Charlie respectively as they ran into his open arms.

Charles looked to Anne for an explanation, which she readily supplied. "Nicholas knocked himself unconscious falling from a tree. As you can see, he's much better." Anne glanced over at Nicholas with a smile. Her young nephew had moved onto dessert, savoring the ice cream bar that followed the completion of his dinner. Anne continued, "The nurse said all of his vitals look good and the doctor should be here shortly." Charles nodded in relief.

Ten minutes later, the doctor arrived. He and Charles stepped into the hall to speak privately. Moments later, Charles came back into the room with a reassuring smile on his face. "Good news! The doctor said Nicholas only incurred a mild concussion, but to be safe, he'll need to stay the night as an extra precaution."

"Oh, that's a relief," Mary said, standing.

Charles looked at his watch. "Well, since Nicholas is going to be okay, I hope you all don't mind if I hit the road? I'm starving. If I head out now, I can still make it to my parent's place in time for dinner."

"What!" Mary said with astonishment, "You can't leave!"

"Why not?" Charles asked. "The doctor said Nick's fine… nothing a good night's rest won't cure." Mary roughly pulled Charles into the hallway as he continued to plead his case. "…and your sister's with you, Mary," Charles said, stating the obvious. "I'd ask you to come too, but I figured you wouldn't want to leave Nicholas. I mean, after all, what use am I here? Besides, I really want to meet this Rick Wentworth."

Mary exploded. "Rick Wentworth! What's Rick Wentworth compared to your own son?"

"Come now, Mary, you know the answer to that! I wouldn't even consider going if the doctor thought Nicholas' condition was serious," Charles said defensively.

"Fine, go!" Mary replied tersely, stomping back into the hospital room, leaving Charles alone in the hallway.

Anne tried to act as if she hadn't been listening, but it would have been impossible to not overhear with how loud their voices were raised. Mary looked quite unhappy as she sat down in her chair with a big 'thump'. Charles appeared a moment later, slightly embarrassed. He kissed Nicholas goodbye, ruffled Little Charlie's hair lovingly and then turned to Anne.

"If you need anything, please give me a call," asserted Charles as he left.

The atmosphere in the room following the departure of Charles was subdued, but Anne knew it was the lull before the storm.

Nicholas' pain medication by now had kicked in, so Anne busied herself with tucking in the sleeping boy before tidying up the room.

"I knew this was how it would be. If there is anything difficult going on, men will be sure to get out of it, and Charles is no different. Look at him! He gets to go enjoy himself and just because *I* am the woman, I have to stay here. What do I know when it comes to medical care? I'm no doctor! I am just as useless as Charles is in that regard," Mary ranted.

Anne tried to make peace. "Nursing doesn't come naturally to men, Mary."

Sulkily, Mary spoke, "Well, it doesn't for me either, but do you see me avoiding my duty? It's just that I don't handle stress well. You saw how hysterical I was earlier. I'm quite exhausted. I hardly know which way is up. What good am I here?"

Anne looked at her sister, amazed at how different they were. Trying to hide the annoyance in her voice, she asked, "Mary, would you be comfortable spending the evening away from Nicholas?"

"Well, if Charles can, why shouldn't I?" Mary justified while blushing slightly. "After all, the doctor *did* say Nicholas was perfectly fine."

Anne looked down, knowing her eyes would betray her disappointment in Mary's un-motherly and selfish nature. Sighing, Anne offered what Mary wanted. "If you wish to go, I'll stay with the boys."

Mary jumped at Anne's suggestion, eager to escape. "Really?" she asked.

Anne nodded. Perhaps it was for the best. If Mary had stayed, Anne was certain the night would have been filled with continual complaints. This way at least, Anne could have some peace and quiet.

Chapter 13

Anne fell asleep in the chair next to Nicholas and Little Charlie. It had been a restless night and Anne knew her appearance would be the worse for it.

The sound of clicking high heels coming down the hospital hallway was like an annoying alarm. She opened one eye and looked at the clock—eight-ten in the morning.

"Rise and shine!" came the shrill voice of Mary.

Sitting up, Anne felt the effects of a poorly slept night. *Boy, Mary's sure up early...no doubt she slept like a baby!* Anne thought crossly. Her joints were stiff after dozing pitifully on the hospital recliner. Glancing at the small mirror on the wall, Anne's suspicions regarding her appearance were confirmed. She looked awful! With hair all amuck and clothes wrinkled, she was a dreadful sight to behold. Stretching, Anne instinctually yawned before heading towards the bathroom.

"You look ghastly!" Mary commented.

Anne grimaced at her reflection in the bathroom mirror and made a half-hearted attempt to repair the ravages of a sleepless night.

"I bought you a croissant and coffee," informed Mary. Anne gave up trying to salvage her appearance and accepted the coffee. The warmth of the cup felt good to Anne's hands. "Has the doctor been in yet?" Mary inquired before taking a bite of her Danish.

"No, but the nurse is certain the doctor will send Nick home today. He was fine through the night." Anne sat back down, exhausted. She glanced over at Mary and could tell there was something her sister was bursting to tell.

"Well…don't you want to hear about the dinner?" Mary breathed with excitement. Anne immediately became alert. She had momentarily forgotten about last night. But before Anne could respond, Mary began to share. "Louise cooked again. Obviously a ploy to try and impress their dinner guest, but she really shouldn't have. The chicken was so tough I could barely cut it. But…the real scoop of the evening wasn't how badly Louise cooked." Mary paused for effect, and then burst out, "It *was* him! Your old boyfriend! Rick Wentworth! He's one and the same! I couldn't have been more surprised! And not only that, he's rather handsome. I didn't remember him being so nice-looking, but then, I only got to see him once or twice since Daddy packed me off to boarding school. I'll tell you one thing though…Etta and Louise sure noticed what a fine specimen he is. The girls ignored me the whole evening. You'd think they'd never seen a man before." Anne tried to look surprised. Mary handed Anne her croissant. "Anyway," continued Mary, "I found out he's an author of all things. Charles told me he's very good at it. He even has a fan club! Can you believe that?" Mary laughed. "Boy! Would my mother-in-law love to see him marry one of her girls! It's so annoying." Mary shoved the rest of the Danish into her mouth, then brushed the crumbs from her hands. "Well, Charles should be arriving soon," Mary added. "Once again, it's me that misses out on everything. First thing this morning, my husband headed back over to his mom and dad's house. Can you believe that? And all because Rick was invited to breakfast. Charles and Rick really hit it off last night. They talked of nothing but hunting and fishing, blah, blah, blah, hunting and fishing."

Mary heard what sounded like Charles' voice in the corridor. To confirm, she walked over to take a quick peek into the hallway only to hurry back to Anne. "Oh my goodness, they're here!" Mary exclaimed in excitement.

"Who's they?" Anne asked, finishing up her croissant.

"All of them! Charles, Louise, Etta, and Rick Wentworth!"

Anne stood up, stunned, the color draining from her face.

Mary swiftly barked out an order, "No! Sit down! We don't want to make it look like we were expecting them." Anne obediently reclaimed her seat. Recalling how she looked, Anne touched her face and hair mournfully, then glanced down to her wrinkled outfit. Meanwhile, Mary quickly positioned herself closer to the boys to look more attentive and motherly. She roused her sleeping children, "Wake-up! Daddy's coming!"

Charles and his entourage entered the hospital room with Louise and Etta quickly rushing to the boys with outstretched arms.

Anne looked up at Rick who didn't appear to notice her. In a way it was a relief, yet at the same time, Anne felt invisible and that hurt. Studying Rick, Anne thought him even more handsome than she remembered. Rick's eyes were still the same vivid sky blue, but made even more so by his tanned face and light brown hair. He wasn't a pretty boy like some of the leading men in today's movies. Instead, Rick looked rugged and strong yet still having a persona of kindness—something that made him all the more attractive to Anne.

"Rick, let me first introduce you to the invalid, our oldest son, Nicholas," Charles waved an arm towards his firstborn. "The other is Little Charlie." Rick smiled a greeting to the boys.

"Tell me about your accident," Rick addressed Nicholas. The sound of his voice made Anne's heart catch in her throat. It brought back a rush of old memories.

"I climbed up a tree and fell," Nicholas answered matter-of-factly.

"Oh...and over there in the chair is my sister-in-law, Anne," Charles said.

Rick turned to look in Anne's direction only to nod nonchalantly. To anyone in the room, no one would have ever suspected that Rick had just been introduced to a woman he once asked to be his wife.

During these introductions, Anne had yet to breathe. With her hand clenched tightly to her chair, Anne slowly began to release her grip, but couldn't ignore the devastation she felt at his unemotional greeting. It was a pain that penetrated deep within and stemmed from Rick's seeming lack of recognition.

"Since the doctor has released Nick to go home this morning, I thought I'd take Rick out to my favorite fishing hole today," announced Charles.

The girls got excited upon hearing this. "Do you mind if we come?" Louise asked.

"We love fishing!" Etta exclaimed.

Charles gave his sisters an incredulous look, then smiled wryly. "I thought you two didn't care for fishing..."

Louise looked at her brother as if to say, *Keep your mouth shut!* Then with an air of feigned innocence, she responded, "Where did you ever get that idea." After scowling at Charles for his betrayal, Louise turned her charms on Rick, gracing him with a beaming smile before adding, "It sounds like a lot of fun!"

Charles relented. "Well, if Rick doesn't mind?"

"Not at all," answered Rick.

"What about me? If they're going, I'd like to go," Mary said to Charles.

Charles glanced up in surprise, "But what about the boys?"

"Oh, Anne can take care of them, can't you Anne?" Mary moved to grab her purse, not waiting for a reply.

Charles looked to Anne for confirmation and she nodded, knowing she hadn't really been given a choice. However, secretly Anne was glad for an excuse to go home. It would give her an opportunity to take a shower...plus have a heart to heart conversation with God. *For one thing, why, oh why, did Rick have to show up when I was looking the worse for wear? This isn't amusing, God.*

Chapter 14

Showered and refreshed, Anne settled the boys comfortably in front of the TV to watch cartoons. She had spent the afternoon trying to keep her energetic nephews somewhat calm, persuading them to stay on the couch while entertaining them with a wide variety of games, coloring books, and puzzles. By the time Anne was finished making homemade soup for dinner, she was wiped out. The sound of the front door opening was never so welcome. Anne peered around the corner just in time to see Mary greeting her sons with a kiss on their foreheads. Anne was back at the stove when Mary joined her in the kitchen.

"How was it?" Anne asked.

"Boring." Mary took a spoon out of the drawer and sampled the savory smelling broth. "At each fishing spot, the men had to test the water, standing there for what seemed like forever. And to make matters worse, Etta and Louise couldn't stop laughing the whole trip, acting like silly schoolgirls. I think it even wore on Rick's nerves and who could blame him! Speaking of Rick, he did eventually admit to knowing you. However, he said you'd changed so much he barely recognized you."

Anne felt as if a dagger had been plunged through her heart. She instantly averted her face from Mary to hide the devastation this remark caused.

71

Mary continued, not noticing the pain that had just been inflicted upon Anne. "I'm amazed at how fast he and Charles have become friends. Men are so much luckier that way... by the way, we're getting together again tonight as well. Is dinner ready?"

Anne nodded. She didn't feel much like speaking or eating. Mary pulled two novelty bowls depicting super heroes from the cupboard and started dishing up soup for the boys as Anne walked away.

Heading straight for her room, Anne struggled to keep her tears in check, finally allowing them to cascade at will as she fell onto her bed. Anne was crushed, all hope wrenched from her. What a fool she'd been! To think she believed Rick when he told her that no matter how much time passed, she forever possessed his whole heart. Obviously, that sentiment must have been contingent on her maintaining her looks! Anne studied herself in the mirror. No wonder Rick barely recognized her; she wouldn't have recognized herself either. She had changed. Anne no longer was the young high school girl from back then. Even Anne couldn't deny the effects age and sadness had caused. Fine lines around her eyes were becoming more evident and the dark circles were getting hard to ignore. Her complexion no longer exhibited a youthful glow. Anne wasn't happy inside and it showed, giving her a tired look. Rick's comment had burned her to the core. If he no longer found her attractive—a man who previously swore undying love—then who would now? Was she destined to become an old maid like both her sisters believed?

Anne hated it when married women or divorcees would try to bring comfort to her single status by confessing marriage wasn't all that it was cut out to be—even going as far to say Anne was actually "lucky" to be spared marriage since it allowed her to do whatever she chose. But what fun is that when you don't have someone special to do things with?

Anne once believed Rick to be the man of her dreams, but yet he hadn't considered her worth fighting for. Anne had been so hurt and disappointed by love that she found her heart hardening towards the idea of romance. With divorce rampant and infidelity common, Anne was almost convinced marriages like her parents' or Carol's were one in a million and something she'd never find. The type of relationship Anne desired could only be found in her favorite books or movies—but those were only fairy tales. Anne had allowed herself to fall for such nonsense when she met Rick. But now…well, she knew they were just lies and falsehoods meant to lead young hearts astray. It was evident Rick didn't want her, and since she couldn't envision herself with anyone else her life seemed destined to be lived alone. *But at least now, the only person who can disappoint me is myself.*

During the past several years, Anne had thrown herself into schooling and work—anything to take her mind off her heartache. She hadn't bothered much with her appearance nor to keep up with the latest trends. Even wearing a little makeup was rare and reserved for special occasions—and those were few and far between. Anne's feminine pride just wished that Rick could have seen her at her best—but then, did it really matter? Rick's reaction, or rather lack of it, was like the closing of a door…the door to her heart, which had still been so open to him.

Chapter 15

Mrs. Musgrove had been busy...busy plotting that is. Her scheme was to invite the whole family out to dinner, as long as Rick was to be one of their party. Clara reasoned that the more time Rick spent in the company of her daughters, the greater the chance he would form an attachment. Anne, upon learning she had been invited, was not keen to attend. She was torn though. A part of her wanted to hole up in her bedroom, drowning her sorrows with Dove chocolates. But another side of her wanted to be around Rick, no matter how much it hurt. Anne attempted to excuse herself from dinner by saying she needed to watch the boys, but Clara would not hear of it. Anticipating Anne's excuse, Mrs. Musgrove engaged a babysitter in advance. So, with mixed emotions, Anne accepted, but this time, dressing in something new and more flattering. At least the evening would give her an opportunity to present herself to Rick in a more positive light.

Arriving at the restaurant, the Maitre d' helped show the party to their seats. Rick, with the prompting of Clara, had also invited his sister and Admiral Croft since the Musgrove's were eager to meet his family upon learning they were in town visiting Rick.

The large group was more eager to talk rather than order, and consequently they delayed in making their food selections. By the time their dinner finally arrived, Anne was famished! She had to keep reminding herself to eat slowly—no way did she wish her eating habits to be a topic of discussion for Rick later!

Mary looked around the popular and trendy restaurant packed with people. It had been rated one of the best restaurants in town, known for its amazing Baby Back Ribs and gourmet salads. "How on earth were you able to get a table here on a Friday night and with such short notice?" Mary asked her mother-in-law.

Clara smiled appreciatively in the direction of the Croft's. "Oh, it wasn't me! At first I couldn't get in! But when I told the Croft's where I'd hoped to go, they managed to somehow secure a reservation!"

Admiral Croft smiled. "I have to confess my wife used some clout...she promised the manager an autographed copy of Rick's latest novel. It worked wonders as you can see," he said while looking at his wife with a twinkle in his eye. Louise, Etta, and Mary all emitted suitable sounds to indicate how impressed they were before returning their attention to Rick.

"What made you become an author?" inquired Louise.

"Therapy," Rick answered bluntly. "It was an inexpensive way to help me deal with a difficult time in my life." Rick's eye momentarily caught Anne's and she blushed, wondering if he was making a reference to their previous relationship. "I found writing to be a helpful outlet...plus, as comes with serving in the Navy, I had a lot of free time at sea, so I just let my imagination run loose. This summer my fourth novel will be released. If I'd known how lucrative writing could be, I'd have started sooner. Speaking of which, this dinner is on me in return for your kind hospitality."

"Rick, that's not necessary," Charles said in close unison with Mr. Musgrove who seconded the sentiment.

Rick, refusing to be deterred, stated with resolution, "Please...I insist. It would be my pleasure."

Knowing it was pointless to argue further, generous thanks ensued from everyone.

"Rick, tell us about your Navy days. What ship were you stationed on?" Etta asked.

Picking up his water glass, Rick settled back into his chair, prepared to reminisce. "I was stationed on a cruiser nick-named the Asp." Rick took a sip from his drink.

"Why the nickname of Asp?" Louise inquired, asking the question on everyone's mind.

Admiral Croft interjected, "Because she was a big pain in the Asp," he chuckled. "I remember that ship well, quite worn out and on its last leg. Rick was part of the final crew to take her out. Hardly fit for service then."

"Did being in the military help you come up with some of the settings in your novels?" Mrs. Musgrove asked.

"Yes. The Navy provided me with the opportunity to travel quite a bit. Plus, the military libraries allowed me to include a lot of historical research. Good thing I enjoy doing both. I usually try to write from a new location for each novel. It helps to not only inspire me, but keeps me busy as well," replied Rick.

Anne sat spellbound as she listened. In the past, she found Rick to be an interesting man, but now time had only served to add to his intrigue. In all the years since dating Rick, she had yet to encounter a man who compared to his personality, character, and fascination.

"But there is a short coming to that," Mrs. Croft warned, "You see, with nothing to tie Rick down, there's no reason for him to stay in one place very long. Although this makes for good novel writing, it's not conducive for family life. I mean, how is Rick ever to meet someone?"

The Admiral gave a merry laugh. "You're in for it now, my boy!"

"Without a wife, a man soon wishes to be on the go again," Mrs. Croft said with a pointed look in Rick's direction.

Rick immediately picked up on it. "Oh, no! Here it comes again!" he said teasingly. "I'm getting out of here before my sister begins her inquisition on why I'm not married and how she wants me to settle down!"

Mrs. Croft sent Rick a challenging look, adding, "And right I should."

Using a flirtatious voice, Etta unexpectedly spoke up. "I'll rescue you," she suggested and Rick looked slightly alarmed. "Oh...I didn't mean...please don't look so worried!" Etta continued, blushing. "I'm just talking about an escape to the dance floor!"

Rick smiled with relief, "Great idea!" He was glad of the offer as it allowed him an excuse to flee from his sister's awkward probing. Etta stood and Rick took her extended hand, leading her to the dance floor. Anne watched as jealousy seized her emotions.

Just then Etta's boyfriend, Chuck Hayter, walked through the restaurant doors. The Maitre d' pointed him in the direction of their party and spotting Louise's familiar face, Chuck made his way over to them. Louise couldn't hide her surprise at seeing him and glanced nervously towards the dance floor.

Chuck greeted Louise and the rest of the group. "Your mom mentioned earlier that you all might be here," he explained.

Louise politely made introductions, motioning to each in their party. "Admiral and Mrs. Croft; Anne; this is Chuck Hayter, a close family friend."

Chuck was a cute but clumsy guy. He had all the right looks, yet unfortunately lacked a strong presence—but he adored Etta, and she seemed to like him too which was enough to endear him to the family.

"Where's Etta?" Chuck asked Louise. This time Chuck followed Louise's gaze just in time to see a laughing and flirtatious Etta on the dance floor with Rick. Chuck looked hurt, and rightly so.

Almost as if she sensed his injured gaze, Etta stopped dancing and looked over to where Chuck stood, seeing him crushed. Chuck stared at Etta with an accusing look, then turned to leave, his hurt quickly being supplanted with anger. Rick glanced between the two, swiftly connecting the dots while noting Etta's anxious face as she watched the young man storm out of the restaurant.

Chapter 16

The fact that Rick was an author somehow made Anne feel more like a stranger to him than the girl he had once asked to marry. Back when they were together, Rick was content to remain a lifeguard at the swim and tennis club. To think he had joined the Navy and became a writer! It made Anne feel the length of their separation like never before. She only wished she could have been part of that season and been able to witness Rick becoming the man he was today. *But what if we hadn't separated? Would he have pursued this course of life?* This question plagued her. Although she was happy for him, it also hurt to think he was able to accomplish these things without her.

She was extremely curious about his life, enough so that Anne found herself the following day entering a small local bookstore in pursuit of one of Rick's books. Making her way towards the fiction section, a female employee walked up to her.

"Can I help you find something?"

"Yes, thank you. I'm looking for a book by Rick Wentworth," Anne answered.

"Oh! I adore his novels! They say he's the next Hemingway," the employee gushed. "Which book are you wanting?" The girl scanned the shelf quickly and pulled out Rick's first two books. She handed them in fast succession to Anne who was only allowed seconds to briefly look at them.

When the store clerk handed her the third and last book, Anne answered, "I really don't know which to choose. Any recommendations?"

"Oh yes!" the employee grabbed the book from the bottom of the stack and placed it on top. "This is his first book and my absolute favorite! Obviously people agree with me 'cause they're making it into a movie!" Impressed, Anne looked at the cover and turned it over to read the book's synopsis. The clerk continued, "It's set back in the late 1700s... or mid 1800s...I can't remember exactly, but anyway...it's about a man who's madly in love with this girl but, tragically her father disapproves." Anne looked up, startled. The girl continued, "She's from a very 'snooty' family who tells the guy to get lost. So, the man joins the British Naval Fleet, thinking that being at sea will—"

"Excuse me, miss..." an intruding customer interrupted. The employee turned to assist the other customer. Anne took advantage of the break to study further Rick's other novels.

After the clerk was done, she turned back to Anne. "Anyway, it's so beautiful...sad, but still terribly romantic." The employee stared off into space and sighed. "I hear he's in town. I would love to run into him. I have this fantasy that if he ever met me, I might inspire his next book."

Anne smiled awkwardly upon observing the employee's enraptured state. *Good grief,* thought Anne. *Do all the young ladies swoon over him like this? It appears I'll need to read his books and find out what all the hoopla is about!*

Unfortunately, Anne's work took priority to that of reading, especially after she had just shelled out nearly eighty dollars for the three books. That meant Anne had to buckle down to keep some revenue coming in. Sitting cross-legged on the ground later that afternoon, Anne was surrounded by her artwork and engaged in conversation with Carol on the phone. "Did you get that design I sent yesterday?" Anne asked.

Carol, back at her desk in Portland, Oregon, began shuffling through Anne's designs to locate the sketches just sent. Finding them, she answered, "Yes, and I like them. However, what would you say to changing the tint to two different shades of pink rather than the blue?" Carol suggested, setting one of them aside. "Pink is really in right now."

Anne picked up her copy of that particular design from the floor to consider the alteration. "I guess so, but I don't know if it will look as good."

"Well, see what you can do and send the revision to me by tomorrow if you can." Carol turned in her chair to look out the window, and added on a more personal note, "How have you been holding up?"

Anne paused. "I'm doing okay."

"And..." prompted Carol, knowing her god-daughter all too well.

Anne responded resolutely. "I think you were right; Rick has moved on. I just need to do the same." It hurt Anne to admit it, but voicing it aloud, and to another person, was the first step to recovery.

Carol shared the same opinion. "It's for the best."

Anne nodded. "Yeah..." Although her mind was in agreement, Anne just wished she could get her heart to comply.

After the phone call with Carol, Anne moved her work downstairs so that she could spend some time with the boys. Mary came into the room to find Anne wedged between Little Charlie and Nicholas, both of whom were coloring.

"Anne, the girls and I are all going on a hike. I want you to come, too."

Anne disagreed. "Mary, I'm right in the middle of something. Besides, who'll watch the boys?"

"Clara said she'd watch them. Please, if you don't come, I'll be bored to death with Louise and Etta."

Anne got up begrudgingly, still resistant. "Where are we hiking to anyways?" she asked.

Mary looked at Anne as if she were having a blonde moment. "Does it really matter? Good grief! We live in beautiful Eastern Oregon...up some hills, I don't know."

Anne tried one more half-hearted attempt to wriggle out of it. "But I don't have anything to wear."

"I'll lend you something. There! No more excuses!"

Anne succumbed and followed Mary to the master suite for some hiking apparel.

Chapter 17

Etta and Louise diligently stretched while Mary tried to fix her wind-tousled hair. Anne was unable to do either of these tasks. She felt too self-conscious and saw faults in herself that others didn't see. The biker shorts her sister loaned her were extremely tight and Anne was sure every cellulite dimple was exposed for the world to see. Raising her arms was no good either, for it exposed her midriff, and although still reasonably trim, it wasn't Anne's favorite feature to show off.

"Hey, isn't that Charles and Rick up ahead?" Mary said, shading her eyes. With horror, Anne watched the two approaching joggers. "Yes, it is!" Mary confirmed.

Anne's grimaced, recalling her appearance. *Great,* she thought, *Another time he can say how bad I look.*

"Hello there! What are you ladies up to?" Charles asked as the men came to a stop beside them.

"We're going on a hike. You're welcome to join us if you'd like," Mary said.

Charles agreed, "Actually a hike sounds much more fun than jogging. What do you say Rick?" he asked, turning to Rick.

"Count me in," Rick answered without hesitation.

"Oh, no," Anne mumbled. *Well, after seeing me in this get-up, Rick will probably be thanking his lucky stars we didn't end up together,* she mused.

Before Anne could object or try to escape, the party began heading onwards with her in tow. Despite the slight chill in the air, Anne took off her sweater and tied it around her hips which provided some rear and mid-drift coverage. Although this somewhat mollified her mortification, she still felt exposed and uncomfortable.

How do I get myself into these situations? Anne thought. This hike was going to be torturous in more ways than one.

Mary struggled on all the hills, slowing the party down. It didn't help either that she took a water break every few minutes. Anne dutifully stayed behind with Mary, using any opportunity to tug at her shorts when Rick wasn't looking.

Rick acted quite the gentleman when assisting Louise and Etta around rocks and large branches, but then neglected his manners when it came time to aide Anne and Mary. Anne felt of no consequence to Rick, which made her want to cry.

"Anne!" Etta yelled, breaking through Anne's thoughts of self-pity. "You've got to see this! I hope you brought your camera!" Anne nodded, patting her backpack.

Once Mary and Anne reached the crest of the hill, they were greeted by an amazing view of the vast wilderness. The sun glowed, creating a magical moment. Anne eagerly pulled out her camera and began snapping pictures.

The overwhelming beauty before her caused Anne to temporarily forget the awkwardness she felt over her appearance. The artistic side of Anne came into action and Rick marveled at watching Anne in her element.

"Hey, Anne! Do you see that home down there?" Louise asked, pointing to a log house surrounded by trees near the lake. "It's the Hayters' place." At the mention of this, Mary took on a sour expression.

Etta looked disconcerted. "Do you think Chuck will be home?" she asked Louise.

Mary rudely interjected, "Why should we care?" This outburst was prompted by Mary's belief that the Hayters were beneath their family socially. As such, Mary was not in favor of Etta dating Chuck.

Louise disregarded Mary's comment and answered Etta, "Why don't you find out?" With that she grabbed Etta's hand.

"I'd like to come too," Charles said. "Besides, I need to use the bathroom. What about you Rick?"

Rick, sensing the discord, declined, "No thanks, I'll pass."

Charles turned to his wife with a look of pleading. Reading his mind, Mary answered, "I am not going down there. I don't care for Chuck or his mother's company."

"Mary, we've known them for years. It would be rude if you stayed here."

"I don't care, I'm not going. Etta, I want you to stay here as well." Mary took Etta's other hand and pulled her towards herself.

In frustration, Charles breathed, "Fine. If you want to stay, stay." He promptly turned and began walking down the hill.

Louise got a determined look on her face and wrenched Etta's hand from Mary's loosened grip, propelling her sister onwards to hurry after their brother.

Mary looked upset. "I can't stand it when people say you have to do certain things just to be polite. I will not go down there. I am my own person. I don't have to go out of my way for anybody, especially people like *them*."

Rick, hearing this, was secretly repulsed by Mary's contempt and obvious prejudice. Anne blushed with embarrassment and was thankful for Louise's return a few minutes later.

"Rick," Louise said, getting his attention. "There's some blackberry bushes not far from here. Do you want to go pick some with me? I bet my mom could whip up a yummy cobbler with them—plus, they might be nice to nibble on while we wait."

Rick looked over at Anne and her sister before answering Louise. "Sure. Some blackberries might really hit the spot right now."

Louise and Rick wandered off. Mary watched them, and then feeling thirsty fumbled around for her water bottle. Raising it to her mouth, she discovered it was empty.

"I'm thirsty, Anne. Do you have any water? I'd like a sip."

Anne opened her backpack and searched around for her water while keeping an eye on Louise and Rick in the distance. She found the unopened bottle and handed it to Mary who gulped it down greedily.

"How long do you think Charles and Etta will visit with the Hayters?" Anne asked.

Mary wiped her mouth. "Knowing the way Chuck and his mother go on and on, it'll probably be an hour at the very least."

Mary handed the water bottle back to Anne. Anne noted it was empty and sent Mary a piqued look as she placed the container back into her sack.

Mary, observing Anne's displeasure, cried out, "Could I help it if I was thirsty? Surely you wouldn't want me to become dehydrated?!"

Anne shouldn't have been surprised. It was so like Mary to only think of her own needs. Had she known that Mary would end up being so inconsiderate, Anne might have taken a sip before sharing her water.

The two sat in silence for a while until her sister got restless. "I'm going to check and see what Rick and Louise are up to," Mary said as she wandered off to find them.

Anne continued to sit there, waiting patiently, though a part of her also wanted to know what Louise and Rick were doing. To Anne, it seemed obvious that Rick found Louise fun and attractive. Anne suddenly felt lonely, ugly, and old. Wrapping her arms around herself, she believed she had nothing to compete with Louise's youthful charms.

After ten or so minutes of these depressing thoughts, Anne realized she needed to relieve herself. Finding some isolated brush where she could be discrete, Anne quickly took care of business, praying the whole time that no one would stumble across her during this awkward moment. After successfully pulling up her borrowed tight biker shorts—which was no small feat—Anne suddenly heard the sound of approaching movement in the brush some hundred yards away and instantly became alert. She hoped it wasn't a cougar. Listening more intently, she slowly began to recognize the voices of Rick and Louise.

As they moved closer, Louise's words were unmistakable. "...no, I don't think she would have gone if I hadn't made her. Although Etta and I are sisters, we are very different. Once I make up my mind, it cannot be changed, whereas Etta must be prodded wherever she goes. If I was in love with a man, nothing would ever separate us." This last sentence was said in a determined voice.

Rick's voice responded, "Wisely said. She is lucky to have you for a sister. Are Etta and Chuck engaged?"

"Practically," Louise replied.

"Then why didn't Mary want to visit with the Hayters?" queried Rick.

At this last question, Louise and Rick were coming into view as they continued walking in the brush below. Anne was now able to see them easily. This revelation made her realize that she was at risk at being seen as well. The thought mortified Anne, knowing that Rick most likely would think she was spying on them, especially since it was something she had earlier wanted to do. Color spread over her face in embarrassment as Anne sunk lower in the brush so as not to call attention to herself. In doing so she almost fell over. Luckily Anne stifled a scream before it escaped her lips and quickly steadied herself.

"Mary thinks they have no class because they don't have money," answered Louise. "She has too much of the Elliot pride if you ask me. Our family can't help but sometimes wish that Anne had reconsidered Charles' offer."

Rick stopped dead in his tracks. "Charles wanted to marry Anne?"

"Uh-huh. But she turned him down. She would have made a wonderful sister. We all adore Anne. My mom thinks it was because Anne only considered Charles as a brother, but my dad believes it was because her friend Carol didn't think my brother was good enough for her."

Rick's face clouded with anger, remembering his own rejection. "Why? Charles has money," Rick said in a tone that rang with slight bitterness.

"Yes, but he doesn't have connections. As far as Carol is concerned, nobody is good enough for Anne. Fortunately for Mary, Carol didn't take any interest in whom she chose to marry."

Anne watched them wide-eyed as they moved out of sight. If only she could read Rick's mind at that very moment. *What must he think about how I also rejected Charles' offer of marriage? Does he even care? Is he jealous? Or is his apparent surprise only because another man actually found me attractive enough to ask me to be his wife?* The sound of Mary stumbling back roused Anne from the questions she was certain she'd never know the answers to.

Chapter 18

When Etta and Charles returned, Chuck tagged along to accompany them for the remainder of their hike.

Rick stole a look at Anne in time to see her extract a water bottle from her backpack for a needed sip of water. He watched as she became frustrated, remembering that Mary had already finished it.

Grimacing, Anne placed the empty container back into her pack. Rick slowed his pace to hand Anne his own water bottle. Anne looked up at Rick curiously and took it, showing surprise and gratitude on her face. Inwardly, she wanted to cry at his thoughtful gesture. She tried not to read into Rick's chivalrous act, but found herself half-elated and half-hoping. *Can it be that despite the long passage of time Rick still holds some fondness for what we once had?* Anne instantly chastised herself for these whimsical thoughts. She was being foolish and leading herself on. What Rick did for her, he'd probably do the same for anyone—simple as that.

Struggling with her wishful thoughts, Anne followed the group to the top of a knoll overlooking a beautiful and serene lake. Ducks swam across its surface effortlessly, prompting Anne to take a few pictures with her camera. Over the gentle sound of the water pressing against the river's bank, the party heard the sound of an approaching boat.

"Look, Rick! It's your sister and her husband!" Etta exclaimed.

Sure enough, the Admiral and Mrs. Croft could be seen coming downstream, maneuvering their craft towards the bank.

"Ahoy there!" Rick said. "What are you two up to?"

Rick's sister smiled in greeting. "Mr. Croft wanted to feel as if he was on the sea again, so I suggested we rent a boat." Mrs. Croft gestured indulgently at her husband.

The Admiral in turn smiled, "Whatever will make Sophie happy." It was evident the couple were still in love after many years of marriage.

"You all look beat. Have you been walking long?" Mrs. Croft asked the group. "We have room for one more in the boat if anyone is tired, isn't that right, Mr. Croft?"

Her husband scooted over, leaving an empty space, and asked, "Who will it be?" as he patted the metal bench.

Rick quickly approached the boat and mouthed an inaudible comment to his sister.

Sophie looked at Anne, and promptly asked, "Anne, why don't you join us?"

Anne looked hesitant at being singled out. "Me?"

"Why, yes. It will save you a good two miles." Anne was indeed tempted as she was tired from the walk.

Rick, sensing her indecision, came over and ushered Anne to the boat before she could refuse. His touch on her back and hand caused her breath to catch. Anne looked back at Rick to see if he had noticed, but he avoided eye contact.

Once settled in the boat, Mrs. Croft asked, "Comfortable?" Anne nodded and smiled in answer to her question.

Anne was still reeling from the feel of Rick's touch on her. She wondered if he'd experienced the same electrifying jolt. In addition, her mind was swirling with unanswered questions. *Why did Rick single me out for the choice ride on the boat? Was it out of concern because he noticed I was exhausted, or was it so he could flirt to his heart's content with Louise after I'd left?*

"Okay! See you back at the Musgrove's," shouted the Admiral. He was ready to be on the move again and with that, pulled the boat away from the shore towards home.

Once they were a distance away from the rest of the group, Mrs. Croft turned to her husband. "So, what do you think about Rick spending so much time with Louise and Etta?" Her question pulled at Anne's heartstrings.

"I think he's come to the realization it's about time to settle down," he answered.

Anne couldn't blame Rick for wishing to find happiness with someone other than herself. After all, she had been the one who postponed the relationship, albeit with much persuasion from her father and Carol. Still, Anne had hoped things would have turned out differently.

Anne had never wanted the relationship to end. Far from it! Instead, she'd fervently hoped that Rick would have stuck around to secure her father's blessing. Under the circumstances, it was no wonder her dad was resistant, considering Rick was just a high school graduate working part-time as a lifeguard. At 20, Rick was content to live from paycheck to paycheck, seizing any free moments for fun. In reflection, Anne understood now why her father and Carol objected. Yet one thing she could not come to terms with was their concept on social standing. That to Anne, was flat out prejudice. However, instead of Rick attempting to gain her father's confidence, he simply vanished from her life.

"Anne, which one do you think Rick likes better?" asked Mrs. Croft. The unexpected question jarred Anne.

Fortunately, the Admiral responded before Anne could even compose herself enough to address the question. "I put my odds on Louise. She is a spirited little thing and rather easy on the eyes."

"I don't know," Mrs. Croft said hesitantly. "I think he'd prefer the disposition of Etta more."

Anne looked away, finding herself depressed. All this talk about Rick with another woman was painful to say the least. She couldn't wait to get home so she could privately break down in tears.

"Yes, but you forgot, she's already got that fellow...what's his name?" Admiral Croft prompted.

"Hayter, Chuck Hayter," Anne answered softly.

"Yes, that's it. Do you remember the way he looked when he caught Etta dancing with Rick at the restaurant? Now, that's a man in love."

Mrs. Croft agreed, "Of course. You are always right, dear." The Admiral and Mrs. Croft shared a special look between themselves and smiled.

Chapter 19

Two hours later, Anne found herself sitting on the Musgrove's couch watching *Sesame Street* while the boys played with their Lego's. She juggled her attention between entertaining her nephews while also semi-listening to Mr. and Mrs. Musgrove as they happily chatted with the Admiral and Mrs. Croft. Anne perked up at every mention of Rick's name which seemed to be constantly paired with that of Louise, a combination that Anne found quite distressing. She tried desperately to tune this part of their conversation out, forcing herself instead to concentrate on Burt and Ernie.

The sound of boisterous noises coming through the front door startled Anne, announcing the return of the rest of the party. Anne felt herself tense involuntarily even though she'd been anxiously awaiting their return, mulling over the reason behind Rick's actions. Anne didn't know whether to be grateful for the quick lift back to the Musgrove's or not. Yes, she'd been tired, but a part of her had wanted to stay just to be in Rick's presence, no matter how painful.

Seconds later, Anne was greeted by Louise who plopped down on the couch beside her, exclaiming, "We're exhausted!" Anne smiled, but found it difficult to keep her gaze from Rick who seemed occupied. Lowering her eyes, Anne took a deep, inward sigh. At times like this, she wished she could shut off all her emotions, then life would be so much easier.

While Charles and Rick found seats, Mary and Etta sat cross-legged next to the boys who eagerly recounted their exciting day thus far with Grandma and Grandpa. Anne found their enthusiasm amusing and ruffled Little Charlie's hair. Glancing up, she caught Rick observing her. Anne felt a shockwave jolt through her body, not realizing her hand was still entangled in her nephew's locks. It wasn't until Little Charlie complained that Anne became aware she had ceased to move. Blushing, Anne pulled away her hand as Little Charlie proceeded to demonstrate to Etta how to properly build a starship.

Mrs. Musgrove, seeing the happy and contented faces around her, decided to test the waters. Clara liked how well Rick fit in with their family and couldn't help but envision him as a future son-in-law. "So, could you see yourself someday living here permanently?" she inquired of Rick, hoping for a positive answer. Her goal was to have Rick settled nicely next door, if at all possible.

Rick pondered the question, resting his chin in his hand. "Actually, yes. What little I've seen of Black Butte I like. I could easily picture myself establishing a home here." Mrs. Musgrove could not hide the delighted smile these words brought to her face.

Mrs. Croft turned to Clara and Anne. "I'm certainly glad to hear him say so! After all, it was Rick who first told us about the Elliot home being for sale in Portland."

Anne's head jerked up at this news. *How had Rick known?!* Anne's mind swirled with unanswered questions, especially why he would even suggest such a thing to his sister and brother-in-law. She studied Rick carefully as Mrs. Croft talked, hoping that perhaps a facial expression would give her some kind of explanation for his actions, but came up empty.

"Now that we have purchased it," began Mrs. Croft again, "He had better stay in Oregon, especially since it's the primary reason we moved here. The Admiral and I wanted to live closer to Rick." She looked at Rick with a mixture of sadness and tenderness. "You see, I wasn't around much when he was growing up, being fifteen years older and then later, being a Naval wife…"

"Well, we will make it up to him now," Admiral Croft said, seeing the remorse on his wife's face. He smiled reassuringly at Sophie, grasping her hand in an effort to bring comfort.

While Rick's sister and her husband shared a special moment, Mrs. Musgrove utilized the silence to further monopolize Rick. "Next week is our annual parade. Do you think you'll still be in Black Butte for that?"

Louise looked hopefully at Rick, awaiting his answer to her mother's question. Anne could sense Louise was already picturing herself hanging on Rick's arm while showing him around town during the festival.

"I'm afraid not. I'm leaving in a few days to see an old naval buddy who lives near the coast." Louise's face fell upon hearing this.

"What stretch of beach?" asked Charles.

"Lincoln City," Rick replied.

"I haven't seen the ocean for a while…it's quite beautiful there," mused Charles.

"Well, why don't you all come then?" Rick suggested, sitting up in his chair. "I'm sure my friend wouldn't mind. And I believe there's still a number of rooms available in the motel I'm staying at."

"Oh! I would love to visit the coast!" Etta said with excitement, dropping the Lego in her hand to give complete attention to that of planning an excursion away from home.

"We can make a weekend of it!" Louise suggested.

"I don't like the beach. Sand gets in everything," Mary said while picking off some extra fuzz from her cardigan sweater. Rather than dampening their spirits, her reply became a green light to the rest of the party who moved forward with Rick's wonderful invitation.

Although Anne could tell Charles was keen on getting away for a few days, he hesitated because of Mary. Her sister clearly showed a distaste for the whole idea, and Charles knew from experience his wife didn't enjoy the coast, especially since Oregon's beaches were notoriously wet and cold.

"You know, it actually might be nice to get away," confessed Charles. "Maybe we could stay just a few days?" He looked pleadingly at Mary, trying to read her reaction.

"Well, we're going whether Mary comes or not!" Louise said with determination, adding, "And Anne will go, too."

Luckily for Charles, it appeared Mary disliked the idea of being left behind more than she hated going to the beach. "I didn't say I *wouldn't* go," Mary said huffily, her resolve quickly fading.

Louise continued, "Plus, it'd be a nice farewell for Anne before she leaves for Napa Valley."

At the mention of this, Rick's head popped up. He seemed surprised to hear of Anne's plans to leave the area. He made a mental note to ask Charles later regarding her situation. In the meantime, he addressed the whole group, "Well, it's settled then. I'll call my friend to let him know."

Louise put her arm around Anne's shoulders and gave her a sisterly squeeze. "You would like that, wouldn't you, Anne?"

Anne turned to acknowledge the question with a smile and a nod. Louise's inquiry caused Anne to study the young beauty sitting next to her. *Louise really is striking*, Anne thought. *And she has a personality to match, too.* Glancing between Rick and Louise, Anne didn't notice any significant partiality on his side, but yet why did he spend so much time with the Musgrove family?

Chapter 20

Anne was getting carsick. Louise, in her eagerness to admire Etta's engagement ring kept impeding Anne's view by her frequent turns from the front seat. And if Louise wasn't looking at the ring, it was to discuss wedding details, making Anne's stomach lurch on the curvy road heading towards Lincoln City. This made Anne wish she had taken the offer to sit in the front seat. While Anne lowered her window for some fresh air, she attempted to keep her eyes fixed on the limited view ahead. The last thing she wanted to do was puke in Rick's luxury SUV—but it would be one way to make him remember her for a long time, at least as long as the stench remained. Despite her queasiness, the thought made Anne almost giggle.

Etta glowed with satisfaction at her sister's admiration over the clarity of the diamond and its elegant setting. Chuck had finally popped the question the evening after the hike. No doubt having Rick in the area was an incentive for Chuck's quick action in proposing. Although battling her carsickness, Anne was truly happy for Etta.

Rick's Lexus provided a smooth ride while covering the three and a half hour drive from Black Butte to the Oregon Coast. During the trip, Anne listened to Etta and Louise, and when consulted, gave her opinion on their ideas for Etta's big day. The bulk of her time though, was spent reveling in the picturesque landscape along the freeway. Once, as Anne glanced ahead to see if Mary and Charles' Subaru Outback was still in sight, she noticed Rick looking at her through the rear-view mirror. Upon being caught, Rick adverted his eyes so quickly Anne began to think perhaps she'd imagined it, but even so, it caused her heart to skip a beat. *I really need to get my emotions under control,* Anne silently reprimanded herself. Anne wondered how she was going to cope once Rick was out of her life, or worse, married to Louise. *Oh, why did Rick have to show up in my life again?*

When the group reached Lincoln City, they collectively agreed to do some exploring before checking into their motel. The day was bright and sunny despite the slight misting of rain on the drive over, so no one felt like giving up the unexpected hours of sunshine in exchange for unpacking. Etta and Louise headed up the troop in their quest to window-shop, and soon the group found themselves in a gift shop. While inside, Anne chose to explore the aisles with her sister rather than to tag along with Louise and Etta. Occasionally, she stole a look at Rick and Charles who had stationed themselves in front of a rotating wire rack to read some humorous greeting cards on display.

"I love it!" Anne heard Louise say from the jewelry counter, diverting her attention from the men. "Don't you think this necklace and earrings will go well with that new dress I just bought?" Louise asked her sister.

Etta nodded and held up another necklace. "How does this color look on me? I've always loved this shade of green, don't you?" Louise nodded affirmatively.

"Hey, Louise, Etta, come look at this," Rick petitioned the girls. They hurried over to glance at the card he wanted them to read. The three chuckled merrily, and Louise looked up at Rick doe-eyed. Anne wished she had been invited to partake in their amusement, for after seeing Louise's open admiration of Rick, she was in desperate need of a laugh herself.

"How cute!" Louise exclaimed, taking the card from Rick with a determined air. "I'm buying it." With that, she strutted over to the cash register where she and Etta purchased the card along with the jewelry they had been viewing.

As they were leaving the shop, Etta halted with a gasp.

"What's wrong?" Anne asked her with alarm.

"Oh! I just realized the necklace and earrings I bought will match perfectly with my wedding colors!" Etta smiled brightly and then promptly resumed walking with a decided spring to her step, feeling quite elated with her recent purchases.

"I think we should start making our way to the motel," Rick said as he looked at his watch. "My friend Harve is expecting us at seven o'clock so that just gives us an hour to get settled in our rooms."

Munching on salt-water taffy purchased earlier, the group reluctantly agreed, leaving behind the beachfront railing overlooking the torrent and rocky sea below.

After getting checked into their rooms, each unpacked, then spent time freshening up before heading over to Harve's place. The drive was just a mere ten-minute excursion from their motel. After parking alongside the neighborhood street, Rick led the entourage down a path to the front porch of Harve's house. Anne instantly fell in love with it. The place was a picturesque beach cottage with clean-cut and simple lines surrounded by beautiful landscaping.

Rick paused before reaching the staircase at the foot of the porch. "Before we go in, I should mention that another one of my Naval buddies, Ben, is temporarily living with Harve. Ben's been hit with some real hard times over the past year. You see, he was engaged to Harve's sister, Francie. Just two weeks before their wedding date, when Ben was overseas, Francie died unexpectedly. As one would expect, Ben took it quite hard. In fact, he's still having a difficult time recovering."

"How sad!" Etta said, the true romantic of the Musgrove family.

Anne couldn't even fathom the heartbreak Ben and Francie's family must be suffering. She swallowed back tears and found herself already feeling a sense of kinship with Ben, a person she had yet to meet.

Rick rang the bell and Harve opened the door with a warm, welcoming smile.

"Wentworth!" Harve exclaimed, grabbing Rick and giving him a manly bear hug.

"How are you, buddy?" Rick asked his friend, chuckling at Harve's enthusiastic greeting.

"Just fine. Come on in, please, all of you," Harve answered as he motioned for the group to follow. Anne watched as Harve interacted with everyone, noticing that although he wasn't particularly the most handsome man in looks, his masculine and well-built frame was the type that women admired and men wished they had. Harve reminded Anne of the classic movie star John Wayne.

The party moved inside where Harve's wife, Melissa, was there to greet them. Her blue eyes sparkled as she invited them to her home with a glowing smile, proving herself to be as equally friendly as her husband. She was a small woman, which served to greater emphasize Harve's tall and muscular frame.

"Nice to see you again, Melissa," Rick said, giving her a hug.

"It's been too long, Rick! Harve and I have missed you," Melissa said, her hand moving to her stomach without thought.

Rick smiled, and then looked down at her pregnant belly, just barely beginning to show. "Have you and Harve chosen a name yet?"

Melissa looked over at her husband with a playful smile, "We're still undecided—but we have a little time yet. I'm only four months along."

Out of the corner of her eye, Anne noticed a man enter slowly from the hallway and assumed it must be Ben. He was shorter than Harve, with dark hair and melancholy looks. She noted that his eyes were marked by a deep sadness.

"Hey, Ben! How are you holding up?" Rick asked, moving to the brooding man. Ben forced a smile as he gave Rick a hug.

Instead of answering the question, Ben shrugged as Harve steered them into the living room. As the group ventured further into the house, Anne's admiration grew for Melissa's decorating skills. The place was darling! With a coastal theme, Melissa incorporated lighthouses, seagulls and other beach items. Deep reds, sailor blue and white tones were used on the walls and in her selection of furniture. It was the perfect place for a beach escape.

"Everyone, please have a seat. Can I get you anything?" Harve asked, playing the part of host perfectly. Before taking any requests though, he first attended to Melissa to make sure she was situated in a comfy chair and wasn't too chilled. It was evident he doted on his wife, especially with her pregnancy.

"I could use a bottle of water if you have one," Mary said, never hesitant to take someone up on their offer.

"That sounds good," Louise and Etta chimed in.

"Okay, anyone else?" The rest of the party shook their heads and Harve exited to the kitchen.

"So, Ben, what have you been up to?" Rick asked.

"I...ah...nothing actually," Ben answered, his reply quieting Rick.

Luckily, Harve came back into the room with the bottled waters, cutting short the awkward moment as he began handing them out. "Here you go..." Harve said as he started to offer one of the bottles towards Mary but hesitated, not knowing her name.

"I'm sorry. I forgot to make introductions," Rick said, chiding himself. "That's Mary." He pointed to Mary who smiled. "Sitting next to her is Charles, her husband." Harve shook Charles' hand. Rick turned his attention towards Louise and Etta. "Over here are Charles' sisters, Louise and Etta, and..." Rick's demeanor changed ever so slightly, "That's... Anne."

Anne noticed Harve give a knowing nod to Rick, and then share a glance with his wife in a manner that made Anne suspect the couple had previously heard her name before. Anne smiled warmly in response to the introduction, thanking Melissa and Harve for opening up their home to them. Both said it was a pleasure and added that any friend of Rick would automatically be one of theirs.

"Well, I don't know about all of you, but I'm starving!" Harve said, rubbing his tummy. The party's eager smiles showed they were all in agreement.

Chapter 21

The dinner plates held an array of stir-fried veggies, seasoned rice, and slices of flavorful lemon-pepper roasted chicken. The meal was succulent and delicious.

"This is wonderful! Who's the chef?" Mary asked, enjoying the food.

"I'm the cook of course!" Harve said proudly.

Rick burst out laughing. Mary couldn't decide if Rick was snickering at her question or at Harve's enthusiastic reply.

However, all was understood when Harve slowly cracked a smile, chuckling as he said, "Nah! Rick knows me better than anyone. I can't cook worth beans, Melissa's the gourmet chef around here."

Rick agreed, "Boy is that the truth! The guy can't even boil water without getting into trouble!"

Harve objected, "Oh, come on! I'm not that bad!"

With a glint in his eyes, Rick wickedly replied, "Oh, really?! I seem to recall a time when we decided to help ourselves to some food in the mess hall..." Just the mention of this caused the two men to chuckle outright, leaving the group hungry to hear more. Rick continued, "We were starving, so Harve and I decided to sneak into the kitchen to make a quick snack."

Harve jumped in, "And we ended up practically burning the whole place down!"

"What do you mean 'we'?" Rick asked. "You were the one boiling the pot of water that ended up setting off all the smoke detectors!" The two shared a good belly laugh.

"Okay—guilty as charged! Man, I'll never forget that night," Harve said as they settled down. "So much for us trying to sneak in quietly! With all the alarms going off, everybody knew about our escapade! We were assigned to KP duty for what seemed like a year afterward."

"I still have nightmares of potatoes waiting to be peeled!" added Rick.

"Where was Ben in all of this? I'm guessing he was probably the ring leader." Louise said in an attempt to include the silent Ben in the fun.

"Oh, he's much too serious for pranks like that. Plus, Ben was always spending time wi…" Rick's voiced trailed off, stopping himself just in time before bringing up the name of Ben's late fiancé.

Harve came to the rescue, finishing Rick's sentence. "…spending time trying to teach us some manners."

Ben attempted to smile, but he knew what Rick was going to say. The melancholy man picked up his finished plate and excused himself. Melissa quickly stood up and started clearing dishes as well, attempting to ease the sudden tension in the room. Harve gave Rick a look that said a thousand words. Rick felt terrible.

As everyone gathered together in the living room after dinner, Ben stood at the window, watching the waves crash on the rocks below. The stormy sea seemed to mirror his own inner turmoil. Anne studied Ben for a while as the rest of the group listened to Rick and Harve's Navy tales. Feeling empathy for the pain he must be enduring, Anne wondered whether there was a way she could comfort Ben during their stay here.

As though sensing her thoughts, Ben came out of his trance and smiled at Anne kindly. Turning back to the window, he quietly spoke—"Who hath not proved how freely words essay, to fix one spark of Beauty's heavenly ray? Who doth not feel, until his failing sight, faints into dimness with its own delight..."—but he could not finish, the pain clearly etched on his face.

Recognizing the poem, Anne continued the next stanza, "...his changing cheek, his sinking heart confess, the might—the majesty of Loveliness?"

"You are a fan of Lord Byron, too?" Ben looked at her with surprise.

Anne smiled and nodded, "Yes. During my sophomore year of college, I took a course on poetry and fell in love with his words."

"What university did you attend?" queried Ben.

"I went to Willamette," Anne responded.

"I planned on going to college, but then I met..." Ben struggled to get the words out and after a moment's hesitation finished with, "...Francie, Harve's sister." Anne looked down in embarrassment, not sure how to react to the tears she saw pooling in his eyes. Ben continued, "We wanted to get married, but I didn't have any money or a decent job. So I told her we should wait, and I would join the Navy. I promised her after the first tour of duty we'd tie the knot..." One tear trickled down his cheek. "I told her we should wait..."

Anne put a hand on his arm as an act of comfort. "Time heals all wounds."

"No!" exclaimed Ben. Then more softly, "No...not for me. You can't understand how it feels to lose someone you love."

At this declaration, Anne interrupted him, "Unfortunately, I do." Anne felt her throat constrict and eyes moisten as she allowed her thoughts to dwell on her mother's death and the loss of Rick's love. It took considerable effort for Anne to talk further, "Still, we have to learn to move on."

After the words left her mouth, she realized how hypocritical they were. *Who am I to give advice when I still haven't gotten over Rick even after all these years?* To see the way Rick acted around her now—Anne could be persuaded he'd never cared to the same extent she had. Sure, Rick was civil, perhaps even kind to her. But there was no partiality towards her in his expressions or gestures. That somehow hurt Anne the most.

Anne knew she should attempt to avoid Rick, especially since it opened her heart to more pain. If Rick were rude or cruel to her, then she could at least grow to dislike him, making it easier for her to cope with her emotions. Yet Rick was still his charismatic, engaging self, which only served to remind Anne of why she was drawn to him in the first place. She would have done anything for Rick, even following him to the ends of the earth, but now it was his loss. The steadfastness and loyalty Anne possessed was not easily found in a woman nowadays.

Just then Rick looked over to see Anne's hand on Ben's arm. Although it was an intimate gesture he surmised Anne, with her compassionate heart, was merely consoling his distraught friend.

Considering his thoughtless words at dinner, Rick was grateful that Anne was now able to provide a measure of comfort to Ben. However, remembering how sweet and tender was Anne's nature, he unexpectedly felt a twinge of jealousy at seeing his friend being the recipient of her kindness. He did his best to shake off the feeling. After all, there was no point dwelling on something long since dead.

The following day, the group took to the beach. Ben and Anne straggled behind the rest of the party, taking their time as they continued to chat and enjoy each other's company.

Rick turned around, only to see the two deeply engaged in discussion and intermittent laughter. He wasn't so sure how he felt about this budding relationship. On the other hand, when it was just him and Louise flirting for Anne to see, it seemed so harmless. Perhaps he had been trying to salvage his pride; being around Anne once again brought back all the old feelings of rejection. Besides, if Anne didn't want him, could he help it if other women found him attractive? Rick's thoughts were interrupted when Louise and Etta requested help setting up the kites they'd purchased earlier.

Anne chose to watch rather than participate. Finding a suitable rock nearby, she sat down and prepared herself to enjoy the kite show. Ben followed Anne, asking if there was room for one more on her perch. Together they enjoyed the havoc below as Etta made several unsuccessful attempts to maneuver her kite with Charles' assistance.

With the wind not cooperating and an inexperienced Etta at the helm, the kite swooped down to chase Mary like an attacking plane. In desperation, Mary was forced to dive into the sand head first to avoid being struck. The embarrassed Etta tried to silence the roars of laughter while Charles swiftly came to Mary's rescue, helping her to get up. After accepting her husband's assistance, Mary shot a nasty look towards Etta, as if her sister-in-law had done it deliberately. Brushing the sand off her clothes, Mary strode off in a huff, followed by further chuckles from everyone except poor Etta who was distressed over Mary's angry reaction.

Chapter 22

The next morning, Anne awoke and glanced at the motel alarm clock which read 6:09am. She told herself to go back to sleep, since after all, this was supposed to be a vacation. But, try as she might, she couldn't sleep anymore. Not only that, but the sound of the waves were beckoning her for an early morning walk, one she hoped she could enjoy in solitude. She got out of bed, headed over to the windows, threw back the curtains, and squinted at the beautiful sunrise.

Dressing quickly, Anne finished pinning up her hair as she ventured down to the motel lobby. As she headed in the direction of the exit closest to the beach access path, Anne passed the continental breakfast table heaped with donuts and Danishes. The smell of pastries was always tempting, but Anne's resistance was fortified by a picture of the extra pounds that always accompanied such indulgences. Onward she trudged, ready to inhale the fresh ocean air, when, to her displeasure, she heard her name being called just as she was pushing the exit doors. Anne turned back to see Etta approaching.

"Are you headed outside for a walk on the beach?" she asked.

"Uh-huh," Anne said, almost hesitant to answer.

"Can I join you?"

Anne nodded an affirmative, doing her best to hide her disappointment. She didn't have the heart to turn Etta down.

Together they trudged along to the beach path walking side by side with Etta talking all the while. Normally, Anne would have welcomed the companionship and idle chatter, but today she would have preferred letting the morning speak all for itself. There was something magical about the early sky along the coastline. Shining brightly just above the vast sea's horizon was the golden sun. It glowed with the morning's warmth, yet the sea brought wet, salty winds. How could something so magnificent as the sun, which seemed so near just then, not protect her skin from the chill caused by the cold wind rushing past? It was a great mystery Anne would never understand, or at least one of them. She didn't want to think about the other mysteries just then, for they pertained to Rick. Instead, she turned her attention back to Etta.

"So Chuck and I are thinking of a late summer wedding. Of course Louise will be my maid of honor, but…Anne, what would you say if I asked you to be one of my bridesmaids?"

Anne was immediately touched. She turned to Etta, giving her a bright smile along with a hug. "Etta, I'd be honored. Thank you!"

"Well, Anne, you're like a sister!" Anne smiled in response. Switching gears, Etta asked, "Do you think I should invite Rick? I think he likes Louise."

With that comment, Anne went from elation to swiftly having the wind knocked out of her. Quickly, Anne tried to recover her composure, telling herself it was bound to happen sooner or later. Anne couldn't respond, not that Etta noticed as the girl continued spilling out her thoughts.

"And, I'm positive Louise will want Rick there. Speaking of which, you seem to be getting pretty chummy with Ben. Is there something happening there?"

Anne was taken aback. Horrified, she wondered if this was everyone's impression, not just Etta's. "Ben? No, he and I are just friends. I…"

"Ah ha!" Etta interrupted, grabbing Anne's arm. "Take a look down there!"

Anne looked to where Etta pointed to see Louise and Rick walking up the beach path together. Her heart was gripped simultaneously with jealousy and pain at the sight.

Etta's eyebrows rose with shrewd enlightenment. "I was wondering where my sister had run off to this morning. Normally she sleeps in until at least ten...well, anyway like I was telling you, Louise's got it bad for Rick, and from what we're witnessing right now, he doesn't seem to mind."

Anne looked away to hide her troubled thoughts, hoping to compose herself sufficiently to pull off an air of indifference for the rest of the day. As for the remainder of the trip, Anne couldn't promise that her heart would comply.

Chapter 23

"So, where's Melissa?" Rick asked as he ascended from his vehicle to join Harve and the others in the parking lot outside the town's favorite local diner. The whole crew had agreed to take breakfast together before hitting the beach later that afternoon.

"Morning sickness," Harve answered apologetically as he scrunched up his face. "She really wanted to come, but breakfast is her number one enemy right now."

"Poor Melissa," Etta cooed as Rick nodded and motioned for them to make their way into the restaurant.

The diner was located just off the main drag and had an incredible view of the ocean. The establishment was famous for their over-easy eggs and succulent French toast, something Anne couldn't wait to devour. After her morning stroll, and the painful sight of Rick and Louise together, she was ready for some comfort food.

As they entered and waited to be seated, Anne took in the quaint setup, noting that the place probably hadn't changed since it opened in the late 50's. Memorabilia covered the walls and the booths looked like they still had the original cushions. As Anne's eyes turned to observe the large breakfast crowd, she did a double take at noticing an attractive, muscular man blatantly sizing her up. His obvious perusal of her caused Anne to blush profusely, so she averted her eyes downward in an effort to ignore him. Anne tried to think of any reason why he'd be staring at her but came up empty-handed. Maybe the stranger thought she'd been checking him out?!? No, that was the first time Anne had laid eyes on him since coming in. Anne quickly did a mental checklist of her appearance, thinking surely, that something must be noticeably wrong to call such attention. Yet, she had taken special care of her hair and face that morning, dressing in jeans and a cute top with a zip-up hooded sweater...so then what could be prompting him to stare so openly at her? Mustering up the courage to look in his direction again, the man dared to cockily incline his head towards her in a nod. Anne was mortified—it was like he had been expecting her to look! Her face burned with embarrassment.

Etta and Louise, who had been observing this exchange, turned to Anne with coy expressions.

"I think Anne has an admirer!" Louise teased.

"I agree," Etta chimed in. "Anne, do you know that guy?" she asked in a hushed whisper.

Anne attempted to shy away from their inquiries, explaining she didn't have a clue as to the identity of the man. It only made matters worse that this humiliating interaction was now being noticed by the whole group, especially Rick, thanks to the girls' excitement at Anne's potential beau. At the realization of the latter, Anne's countenance brightened somewhat. To think Rick was a witness of this was like balm to her wounded soul. Although Anne didn't usually like to be singled out this way, at least Rick was there to notice that a man could still find her attractive.

Unwittingly coming to Anne's rescue, the waitress finally arrived and led the party to a booth overlooking the sea. Anne didn't dare look back to see if the stranger was still perusing her as she walked to the table, but she found it almost impossible to walk normally knowing he might be staring. Her gait felt awkward and her arms just seemed to dangle doing nothing—should she move them? Clasping them together, she scooted into the booth first, sitting next to the window with her back to the entrance, and more importantly...*that* man. Rick scooted down the bench opposite her, and Anne watched as Louise made sure to secure a seat next to him. She also watched wearily as Ben took great pains to sit next to her. She didn't want to hurt this already heartbroken man, but on the other hand, she didn't wish to encourage him either. Luckily for her, Anne now had the menu to prop up in front of her fading red face. This allowed her some privacy as she took deep breaths and alternately applied cold hands to each cheek. By the time Anne lowered the menu to tell the waitress what she wanted, her appearance and composure were almost back to normal. The waitress took away Anne's "security blanket", aka the menu, and promised to return soon with their food.

"What do you all think about visiting the sea lion caves after our time on the beach?" Charles suggested to everyone's delight.

"Oh, too bad the boys aren't here," Mary said to Anne's surprise. Sadly, it was rare when Mary missed her sons, which deeply disappointed Anne at her sister's lack of maternal instinct. Perhaps now that the boys were getting older her sister's attachment to her children was growing. Anne hoped that was the case.

"Sure, I wouldn't mind," Rick said shrugging as he took another sip of the hot coffee the waitress had refilled before she left.

Louise began to recount a past experience with a sea lion during an internship she held at a sea life aquarium two summers ago, much to the enjoyment of the group. Her story was cut short though when a waitress from the counter called out, "Order to go for Will Elliot!"

The familiar sounding last name caught the group's attention and collectively they turned to see who would claim the food. Lo and behold, the same man who earlier had been checking Anne out approached the counter to receive the order.

"Anne…are you thinking what I'm thinking?" Mary asked Anne dramatically.

"Do you know him?" Rick queried, trying to curb the jealous twang in his voice.

"Not him personally," Anne responded, a little surprised at Rick's latent displeasure. "Our family is related to someone with that name. The 'Will Elliot' we've always heard about is a second cousin, once removed or something like that. Elizabeth—"

"That's our oldest sister," Mary interjected quickly.

Anne grimaced, knowing Mary was getting excited to embark on some family gossip. Continuing where she left off, Anne began again, "Well, our sister used to date him when the two of them attended Dartmouth together."

Anne was not surprised, when once again, Mary interrupted.

"That is, until Will found someone richer and married her! The woman's inheritance made Daddy's fortune look like nothing! Sadly, we never got to see what the 'rat' looked like though, since Elizabeth wanted to keep the guy all to herself. The only ones who got that privilege were Dad and Mrs. Russell when they visited Elizabeth at college."

"Needless to say," continued Anne amused, "My family is not on good terms with him."

"The name is certainly a coincidence, but it's probably a different guy," Charles advised, bringing the discussion to a close as they saw their food approaching.

Anne continued to observe Rick as he received his plate of pancakes while still maintaining a visual on the stranger. She wondered what Rick must be thinking. *Is he just curious about the coincidence, or is he a little jealous?*

Rick was glad when he watched the stranger finally exit the restaurant. Now that Anne's admirer was out of the picture, he could turn his full attention to breakfast. Yet, while taking the first mouthful of the delicious pancakes set before him, Rick couldn't quite understand the jealousy he felt at seeing another man admire Anne.

Anne, slicing a piece of her syrup-sweetened French toast, was also reflecting on the stranger. She had assumed the man at first was merely appreciating her looks, but now knowing he could possibly be her sister's ex-boyfriend, wondered if his interest was because of a resemblance to Elizabeth. If so, that would be a first. No one had ever remarked on the two of them looking similar, in fact, quite the opposite. Well, so much for her ego. Surely now, knowing his name, it would explain his keen observation of her. Her growling stomach took priority over further pondering, and she put aside the thoughts for later.

Chapter 24

The Oregon Coast, although beautiful, was normally a little chilly. Today was no exception. The group sported sweat-shirts and jackets to fend off the cold breeze as they enjoyed some time on the beach.

"Anne, I can't begin to tell you how much I've enjoyed our conversations," Ben said as the two of them sat talking after breakfast on top of a dune.

The others were playing Frisbee below on the sand, with the exception of Mary who elected to read the latest *Enquirer* (she wasn't much for games), and Harve, who had earlier sprained his ankle.

Anne responded to Ben politely, "I've also valued our chats." Anne did her best to keep her tone reserved. Although she thought her answer appeared neutral, Ben's confidence was boosted by her response so he continued.

"We really do have a lot in common," he said, searching her eyes for any hint of coinciding passion.

With the sun shining behind him and into her face, surely the only thing Ben was bound to see were reddened eyes. The combination of wind, rain, and light were making them irritated and painful. In fact, they were already begin-ning to water. Instinctively, Anne pulled her jacket tighter around herself. She wasn't sure if it was because of the icy gust of wind that blew upon them at that moment or rather the nagging feeling which told Anne she needed to tread cautiously.

The way Ben was gazing at her made Anne feel distinctly uncomfortable. She recalled Etta's words asking if the two of them were an "item" and with today's pointed admiration from him, Anne could no longer delude herself that Ben simply thought of her as a friend. The notion unnerved her.

"So you're moving to Napa Valley?" Ben asked. Anne nodded, striving to make her answers seem nonchalant. Without warning, Ben eagerly grabbed Anne's hand. Startled, Anne sat in shock at Ben's next revelation, "I've been considering a move to California myself," he ventured, no doubt hoping to spark an outburst of joy from her lips.

Anne tensed, but was saved from responding when they heard Rick call out to Louise in alarm. She took this distraction as an opportunity to take back her hand. Ben looked a little injured, but to Anne's immense relief, the commotion below caused him to overlook the slight.

"Louise! Not so far out!" Rick shouted.

Despite his warning, Louise continued to walk backwards into the shallow surf, shaking her head playfully as she did so. "What?" taunted the flirtatious Louise, "Afraid you won't be able to throw the Frisbee this far?"

Anne sighed. Sometimes that girl could be so headstrong! The foolish Louise regressed further into the sea water while continuing to motion for Rick to throw her the disc. Goaded, he tossed the Frisbee to her and she caught it.

"Louise," Charles sighed with annoyance. "Don't be an egghead! Come back now."

Stubbornly, Louise refused as the icy waves slapped against her legs. Spying a large boulder exposed by the receding waters, she chose instead to hoist herself onto it. Once reaching the peak, she flauntingly waved the Frisbee.

"Louise, get down from there! The tide is starting to come back in," Rick said, his voice displaying his annoyance.

Louise's only response was to continue laughing, despite the concern plainly written on everyone's face. This was her day to shine, and Louise reveled in the attention she was receiving.

Ben's touch on Anne's arm caused her to look away momentarily from Louise's daring antics only to hear Etta, seconds later, let out a horrifying scream.

"Louise! Watch out!" Mary shouted.

Anne looked back just in time to see a sneaker wave crashing over the boulder, knocking Louise off her perch. The party stood helpless as they watched Louise fall and strike her head on a jagged rock before sinking unconscious into the rushing water below. Bursting forth, Rick plunged himself into the mighty waves, jumping in after her.

"Oh, dear God!" Anne said with a shaking voice as she got up and ran down to join the others with Ben following close behind.

By the time they reached the scene, Rick had managed to grab Louise and was barely holding onto a protruding crag on the face of the boulder. His grip, although not totally secure, was just enough to stop them from being swept out into the ocean by the strong current. Anne felt as if she was watching a horror movie. She wished she could push "stop" and rewind this moment to keep Louise from being harmed. Instead, all she could do was stand there helplessly, and pray to her Heavenly Father for a miracle.

As soon as the water partially receded, the men sprang into action. Charles, Ben, and even the injured Harve helped to take the unresponsive Louise from Rick, and despite Harve's sprained ankle, the trio managed to get her to safer ground. Anne was the only one who offered the soaked and exhausted Rick a shoulder to lean on which he accepted with gratitude as he staggered to safety.

The group straight away surrounded Louise with Charles dropping to his knees to cradle his lifeless sister. Anne assessed the situation and realized immediate medical attention was needed. Unlike Mary who was hyperventilating, Anne instinctively put her first aid skills to use, pushing aside the others to lower her head onto Louise's chest to listen for any sign of life. Thinking she heard a slight beat, she placed her ear above Louise's mouth to confirm.

"She's breathing!" Anne cried out with relief. Etta gasped and steadied Mary, who was close to fainting.

"What should we do?" Charles asked, his voice quavering with emotion.

"We need an ambulance," Anne ordered, sensing the men needed direction.

Out of the corner of her eye, Anne watched as Rick struggled to rise. It was only then that she realized he, too, was badly hurt. Catching sight of oozing blood coming from some cuts on his hands, Anne stopped Rick before he could rise further. She placed a gentle hand on his shoulder which caused him to flinch. Horrified, she recognized that his shoulder was dislocated and now felt guilty for the discomfort the slight pressure had caused him.

"Rick, you're hurt!" she said with concern, "Let Ben make the call."

Rick recognized the wisdom of her words. He nodded to Ben who ran off with determination and speed, heading to where the group had left their belongings so he could retrieve his cell phone.

Forcing herself to once again focus on Louise's more serious condition, Anne turned back to the unconscious young woman. Louise's arms and legs were ice cold, putting her at risk for hypothermia.

"It's vital we keep her warm," Anne said with alarm, prompting Harve and Charles to quickly take off their jackets and sweatshirts. Anne accepted them and promptly laid the donated items over Louise.

Rick attempted to raise his arm with little success, grimacing with extreme pain. He paused, his eyes betraying his anguish and wretchedness. "Anne, I should have stopped her..."

"It's okay, it wasn't your fault. Louise can be so head-strong at times," Anne answered in an effort to soothe his conscience.

"But, I should have been more forceful..." Rick objected.

Anne stopped him. "And do you really think that would have worked on Louise?"

Rick sunk back in resignation, knowing that Anne was right. There was nothing he could have done to stop the willful Louise.

"But we can pray," Anne prompted, turning to massage Louise's cold limbs in an effort to keep them warm.

Rick and the others nodded in agreement to Anne's suggestion. A peace descended over the group following Anne's gentle reminder that God was in control. Each knew that Louise's fate rested solely in their Heavenly Father's hands.

Chapter 25

White walls and medicinal smells surrounded them as they huddled together in the cramped hospital room. All the faces present displayed concern, except for the motionless and unconscious Louise, whose lovely face was without expression. Once the doctor had declared Louise's condition stabilized, Charles was able to secure permission from the hospital staff to allow the entire group to be in her room. Normally this wouldn't have been possible, but since it was an outpatient facility the staff had been able to bend the rules a bit.

As they stood around waiting for the doctor's return, Anne shouldered the task of bearing the bad news to the Musgroves. Normally Charles would have undertaken this duty, but he was busy trying to keep Mary and Etta from hysterics. Once the call was initiated, Anne had to wait patiently for Clara to calm down sufficiently for her to continue. She glanced at Rick, glad to now see his injuries properly bandaged and a sling in place. It had been a close call, and granted, Louise wasn't totally out of danger yet, but at least she was alive and currently receiving proper medical attention.

In the background, she could hear Mr. Musgrove coaxing his wife to hand over the phone. "How is she, Anne?" Stanley asked with such gravity that a lump formed in Anne's throat.

"She's in stable condition. They took some x-rays earlier and we're waiting to hear back from the doctor regarding the results."

"Has she said anything? Is she awake?" he asked, trying to maintain his composure.

"No, she's still unconscious," Anne began, wishing she had better news to share. "The only thing we know at this point is Louise suffered a concussion and appears to have a broken wrist and collar bone."

This discourse was interrupted when the doctor entered Louise's room. Promising to ring Stanley later with the physician's update, Anne quickly ended the call. Everyone's eyes turned hesitantly to the doctor as they waited for him to speak.

"Well, all the neurological tests came back negative," he began, which emitted grateful sighs of relief throughout the room. Anne quickly sent a prayer of thanks to God. The doctor continued, "Louise is showing normal brain activity at this point, but until she regains consciousness, all we can do is wait. Personally, I view the unconscious state as the body's method of attempting to heal itself," the doctor explained, trying to soothe the worried faces.

"How long do you think she'll be unconscious?" Charles asked.

The doctor shifted, placing Louise's chart under one arm. "Could be days, maybe even weeks. There's really no way to tell. The biggest hurdle now is to watch for increased cerebral swelling." Charles nodded gravely and the physician added, "As we suspected, her collar bone and wrist were broken in the fall. In addition, she has a fractured hip."

At this announcement, Etta and Mary began to wail. Anne felt concerned too, but decided the better option would be to find solace in her Heavenly Father. What good would crying do? She decided to save her tears for later. What this group needed now was strength, and even though she felt weak, Anne knew she had to be strong for Louise.

"Is there any way we can move Louise to a hospital closer to Black Butte?" Charles asked, eager to relocate his sister so she could be nearer to their worried and distraught parents.

"That, I would not recommend. What she needs now is consistency," the doctor explained.

Although disappointed by the doctor's response in moving the patient, the group understood that Louise's health was top priority. If keeping her at this present location would increase Louise's chances of a full recovery, then so be it. The doctor left and promised an update later that night, if his rounds permitted.

As evening began to close in and there was still no update regarding Louise's condition, Anne offered to get coffee for those needing a good dose of caffeine. None of them knew how long they would have to remain at Louise's bedside, but felt it would be best to wait for the doctor's recommendation before making further arrangements. Unfortunately, Louise's physician was completing a double shift, having been swamped with an influx of new patients. Since the doctor wasn't expected any time soon, Anne figured this would be a good opportunity to get the offered coffee. Even Anne was finding it a challenge to keep her eye lids open while watching *Full House* reruns, a program which Mary had found on the television. Gathering her purse to embark on this errand, to Anne's surprise, Rick handed her a twenty dollar bill to cover the tab.

"No, thanks. I've got it," she said, softly pushing his hand away. Rick was too exhausted to fight her and reluctantly accepted her decision as he fell back into his seat.

Anne studied his face and distraught manner. *Is Rick overly dismayed because he's exhausted like everyone else? Or is it because his heart is being torn to shreds watching Louise lie lifelessly on the bed?* Anne pondered these depressing thoughts as she made her way to the hospital café and ordered three coffees. Rick's actions earlier that day had impressed Anne though. Despite the pain he'd physically endured during the rescue,

Rick never complained once, even assisting the ambulance technicians as they carried Louise's stretcher up the beach path.

Once the purchase was made, she headed back to the room, only to hear raised voices as she was nearing the door's entrance. The group appeared to be in the midst of what sounded like an heated conversation. Deciding it best not to interrupt, she chose to wait outside until the coast was clear.

"I don't want Louise staying here alone," Anne heard Charles say, "Rick, would you mind driving Anne and Etta to Black Butte and then bring back my parents? At their age, I don't trust them to drive right now, especially with them being so worried."

"Of course, but I really think Anne should be the one to stay," replied Rick.

Rick's comment caused Anne to freeze. Fearing her knees might lock on her, Anne rested against the wall while continuing to unashamedly eavesdrop. She was hoping to hear Rick say more, but instead Mary's upset voice came next.

"What do you mean by that? Anne is *nothing* to Louise. *I*, on the other hand, am her sister-in-law!" argued Mary, obviously disgruntled about the suggestion that she be the one sent home.

Mary's attitude exasperated Anne. Everything was always about Mary. Her sister rarely every considered what was best for the group. Anne leaned her head against the wall, silently venting her annoyance until an unexpected shrill phone rang loudly at the nurse's station, startling Anne's already shattered nerves. Jerking upright, Anne nearly spilt all the cups of coffee on the tray she was carrying. Anne was fortunate that she was able to recover her composure just in time to pin her back against the wall, albeit awkwardly, which steadied the filled cups of coffee. Surveying the floor, Anne was pleased to find that very little liquid had dropped to the ground. Her balancing act was working until Anne realized she was stuck. During her masterful recovery, her feet had distanced themselves nearly three feet into the hallway, leaving her in a precarious position. She knew that any sudden movement could cause her to be upended and all would be lost—surely someone from inside the room would hear the crash of her fall and know that Anne had been listening in on their conversation. Feeling her legs ache and tremble as they fought against the uncomfortable position she was maintaining, Anne had to make a quick decision. Hoping that mini steps back towards the wall might help relieve the pain and regain her balance, Anne slowly began this task. Instantly, Anne felt the strain to her muscles slightly diminish. She began to believe all was safe until one of her shoes came into contact with a bit of the spilt coffee, causing Anne's left foot to slip out of control. Foreseeing herself doing the splits, Anne elected the less painful of the two and chose to let her bottom cushion the inevitable fall. Anne muffled an exclamation of pain as her rear came crashing down with a loud thump on the floor. The noise aroused the attention within the room.

"I just heard something," Charles announced. "Maybe it's the doctor."

Anne was aghast, unsure of what to do next. As Charles moved towards the open hallway, she panicked. Giving herself no time for second guesses, Anne surrendered the tray, leaving it temporarily on the floor so she could stand up unhampered. Knowing she had mere seconds, Anne quickly retrieved the beverages, then moved swiftly several paces away to make it appear as if she was just approaching the room.

"Yes, but I believe Anne the more capable..." Rick said, continuing his point with Mary. In his mind, Mary would be more work than help, creating an extra burden which no one needed at this time.

"I am just as good as she is!" Mary responded in an affronted tone.

Positioning herself in a walking stance, Anne greeted Charles just as he stepped out into the hallway. Overly bright, she said, "Hi Charles, here's the coffee!"

Somewhat surprised, Charles expressed his thanks and motioned her into the room, "We just started discussing who will be staying here to watch over Louise."

"Oh," Anne said as she followed Charles inside.

Mary gave Anne a scowl, then moved in defiance towards Charles as if to say, *Who are you going to choose?*

Anne brushed off her sister's rudeness and handed one of the coffees to Charles and the other to Rick, smiling at the latter as she did so. Anne hoped her smile might convey a measure of her appreciation, knowing that she'd probably never get the chance to personally thank him for his confidence in her. Rick reciprocated the smile, unaware that Anne had overheard his kind words. Immediately Anne was transported back to a time when special looks between the two of them came so effortlessly. It felt so wonderful to once again lock eyes with Rick and be able to truly smile. Savoring these warm thoughts, Anne sat silently while the arrangements were sorted out concerning who would stay.

Mary fought bitterly to the end and achieved victory. No one could really blame Charles though for giving in. What choice did he have? If he didn't let Mary stay, he'd be in the doghouse all week, maybe even longer. Pressing the point just wasn't worth the cost for him, and since he would remain behind as well, Charles felt his contribution in caring for his sister would be enough.

Rick was not pleased about the arrangements but he managed to keep his mouth shut. However, upon observing the triumphant look on Mary's face as she ordered a late dinner for Charles and herself, it became more than he could bear. Rick decided he needed to get away before he said something he'd regret, so he quickly offered to head out immediately with Anne and Etta en route to Black Butte.

Anne had to admit she was a little nervous about the trek back to the Musgrove's. Etta was already having trouble staying awake as it nearly one o'clock in the morning, and that meant she and Rick would essentially be alone for nearly three and a half hours. *Will he try to talk to me? Should I pretend to be asleep?* Anne's thoughts hounded her as she and Etta followed Rick to his vehicle. *I'll just have to follow his lead,* Anne concluded, knowing that this was much easier said than done.

Chapter 26

Anne sat in the back with Etta who, just as she had predicted, was fast asleep. The sound of the steady rainfall outside plus the heat radiating from the vehicle's vents was making it difficult for even Anne to stay awake. But she wouldn't allow herself that luxury, not with the possibility of Rick opening up to her. Several times she fancied Rick looking at her through the rear-view mirror, but then told herself it was just wishful thinking.

"Anne," Rick's velvety deep voice jolted Anne from her daydreaming. Hearing the tenderness in his voice as he spoke her name caused her heart to flutter like that of a middle-school girl with a crush. *Get a hold of yourself!* she scolded. Before Anne could think of how to reply, Rick began again, "I regret..." but then paused.

Yes? Anne thought, hoping she could mentally will Rick to speak more swiftly. *What do you regret? Please tell me!*

But before Rick could finish, Etta stirred awake. Anne watched as Etta slowly raised her head from Anne's lap and stretched. Yawning, she asked, "How long have I been asleep?"

No one answered. Both Rick and Anne were silent, with Anne feeling quite frustrated at Etta's ill timing. *What had Rick planned to say?* So many thoughts raced through her mind. *If the topic had been about Louise, couldn't Rick have con-*

tinued his words? So, if the subject was not about Louise, then what does he regret?

Etta took their silence as a hint, sensing the awkwardness in the air. "Did I interrupt something?" she asked, looking between the two.

"No...nothing at all," Rick answered.

Anne lowered her eyes at Rick's response. She tried to tell herself she was being stupid for feeling hurt by Rick's curt and emotionless reply to Etta. Once again, Anne had foolishly dared to dream that just maybe Rick wanted to make things right between the two of them. *Perhaps Rick regrets his actions which tore us apart—like driving off in anger as he did all those years ago. Or, and this is more likely,* Anne thought ruefully, *Did he just want to apologize for the past before moving on to the future with Louise?* All that they once shared as a couple was now evaporating like a fleeting whisper. Anne began to feel perhaps all she'd ever meant to Rick was just what he had stated to Etta, "nothing"—not even worth the time for him to finish his thoughts out loud.

Anne closed her eyes tightly as if to somehow shield her heart. The solace of a room to herself could not be fulfilled soon enough...

Chapter 27

As expected, the Musgrove home was in an uproar. Mr. Musgrove moved about the house like a man on a mission, all the while trying to placate his incapacitated wife who sobbed on Anne's shoulder. Clara unfortunately assumed the worse about Louise's condition. In Mrs. Musgrove's mind, they had little time left to see their baby girl alive one last time. It took all of Anne's emotional sensibility to soothe Clara's sorrows and assure her that Louise's doctor and the nursing staff had everything under control.

By the time Mr. Musgrove and Rick had loaded up the luggage into the vehicle, Clara had composed herself enough to put on her jacket. "Are you sure you'll be alright?" she asked while embracing Anne at the front door. Clara was worried about Anne having to take care of the distraught Etta and the boys on such a windy and rainy night. That's what Anne admired about Mrs. Musgrove—even in her own trials, she still managed to be concerned for others.

"Yes, now go! Your daughter needs you," Anne assured her.

Mrs. Musgrove kissed Anne's forehead. "Anne, I am so thankful you're here."

Mr. Musgrove opened the front door and stepped part way through, stopping to ask his wife, "Ready, dear? Rick's waiting."

Mrs. Musgrove nodded and walked past her husband as he held the door open for her. Stanley lingered though, hoping he could speak with Anne privately while Clara made her way to the car.

"Anne, I also just want to thank you. Clara feels so much easier knowing you're in charge. Here's the number to my cell phone if you need to reach me." Anne smiled and grasped his hand in a sympathetic squeeze while taking the slip of paper offered by Stanley. With that, Mr. Musgrove gave Anne an appreciative nod and closed the door, carrying with him the final piece of luggage.

Anne went to the window to watch as Rick took the suitcase from Mr. Musgrove and packed it into the trunk. To her surprise, Rick gave one last look in the direction of the house before making his way to the driver's seat to climb quickly inside. Moments later, the vehicle pulled away in the direction of the freeway.

"Is Aunt Louise going to be okay?" Nicholas asked Anne the following evening when she was tucking him into bed next to his brother.

Pushing Nick's hair away from his face tenderly, Anne answered, "The doctor's are doing everything they can to make her better. If you'd like, we can say a little prayer for her."

The boys melted Anne's heart when they immediately put their hands together and bowed their heads. Anne closed her eyes in response.

"Dear God," began Nicholas, "Please make Aunt Louise better. Amen."

Anne smiled and ruffled his hair, "Okay you two, it's time for bed now."

The boys scooted under their sheets and Anne tucked them in, leaning over to kiss them on their foreheads before turning out the light. As she was leaving the room, Anne took a moment to say her own quiet prayer for Louise.

Two days later, Anne sat at the kitchen table sketching some card designs while Etta took the boys outside for some needed playtime. It was good to see Etta coming out of her depression. Being so close to Louise, she had done little more than cry and sleep, worrying so much about her sister since leaving Lincoln City. Looking outside the window, Anne viewed her nephews' intent faces as they played in the sand box with their Tonka trucks, causing Anne to smile. It was refreshing to finally be able to relax somewhat. Since arriving, Anne had been up early each day making calls and doing household chores. With Etta unable to help, it left Anne to shoulder the responsibility of taking care of the boys and being the family's cook and bottle washer—so having this time to finally express herself creatively was a reward for her.

Ten minutes later, the sound of a ringing phone broke her concentration. She got up quickly to answer it.

"Anne, she's awake," Charles said on the line with obvious relief. Anne bowed her head and thanked God for this answered prayer.

Chapter 28

With Louise recuperating nicely, life returned somewhat to normal and Anne found she was not needed as before. The doctor had insisted that Louise stay one extra day at the hospital before moving to the rehabilitation care facility. Louise would require treatment for six weeks while her collarbone, hip and wrist mended. Since Harve's wife, Melissa, was a physical therapist, the Musgrove's felt safe in trusting Louise to her care, and opted to have their daughter treated in Lincoln City. As an added plus, they felt the ocean air would be of benefit to Louise.

Now that everything was stable, Anne was free to join her father in California. With a sense of anticipation that was also mingled with mixed emotions at leaving, Anne packed up her bags and boarded a plane headed for Sacramento.

She found herself humming the old Peter, Paul and Mary tune, "I'm Leaving On A Jet Plane". Anne only remembered a few snippets of the lyrics, but quickly found she was depressing herself with the song as it brought Rick to her mind. *Why does he have to enter into everything I do? How pitiful is that!*

Putting on her headset, she flipped through the selections on her iPod until she came across the newest album from Corinne Bailey Rae which Anne had recently purchased online. Settling back into her seat, she closed her eyes with a determination. *Enough of Rick! It's time to start dreaming of*

my new life in California. What is the saying? 'California or bust!'
With that, Anne resolved to enjoy the flight.

Having arrived safely, Anne shaded her eyes from the blinding sun as she hailed an approaching taxi once outside the airport terminal. Although she had notified her family in advance of her arrival, no one had been there to greet her. Earlier Anne had tried paging them, hoping they might have been running late or perhaps accidentally showed up at the wrong bagging area. But sadly, time had proved each theory wrong. After collecting her luggage and making her way up the escalator into the warm California air, Anne tried hard to hide the disappointment and hurt she felt.

Anne was used to doing things on her own. Since her mother's death at thirteen, Anne quickly discovered if she wanted something done, she had to do it herself. Her father had been too wrapped up in his own life or in Elizabeth, his favorite child, to take notice of her. Although Carol had tried to fill her mother's shoes, for which Anne was grateful, no one could ever replace her mother. Anne and Carol had forged a special bond, yet it wasn't the same, nor was Carol as readily accessible as a real mom, what with her living in a different household than that of the girls.

When the taxi pulled up the driveway to her family's new home, Anne found herself pleasantly surprised. She couldn't help but admire its quaintness, especially since it was surrounded by acres of beautiful and well-kept vineyards farmed by local wine merchants. Anne paid the taxi driver and lugged her suitcases into the house using the key her father had sent her months ago.

"Hello? Anybody home?" she called out while visually taking in her new surroundings.

Glancing around at the tasteful selections of wallpaper, the rich and deep hues of various paint combinations as well as the expensive appointments and exquisite furnishings, Anne instantly recognized her sister's impeccable taste.

Wow! thought Anne. *My sister sure didn't lose any time in redecorating! What a waste that Elizabeth doesn't use this God-given talent to be an interior decorator.* Anne was quite proud of her sister's obvious talent. Elizabeth had done a excellent job incorporating local Venetian influences and blending them into the home's modern style.

Leaving her luggage in the hallway, Anne meandered into the kitchen to see more of the impressive stylistic changes by Elizabeth. A note lying on the shiny marble countertop caught Anne's eye. Picking it up, she read it out loud.

Anne,
Glad you got in safely. Sorry we weren't there to meet you at the airport, but there was an important event at the country club which Dad and I wanted to attend. We'll be back in time for one of your delicious home-cooked meals. Elizabeth

Feeling a bit like Cinderella, Anne raised her eyebrows as if to say, *What a nice welcome home.* Checking through the kitchen's well-stocked cupboards to see what there was to work with, Anne pondered the "important event" that kept her family at the country club. If she was the betting type, which she wasn't, Anne would place her money on a massage for her father and a facial for Elizabeth.

Chapter 29

"How was your time with Mary?" Elizabeth asked Anne later that evening. Her family, along with Susan Clay, were about to partake of the meal Anne, aka Cinderella, had slaved over earlier.

Using the ingredients on hand, Anne prepared chicken, stuffed with feta cheese, along with a savory potato and green bean salad and freshly baked bread. Even Anne was pleased by how well everything had turned out. Reaching for her water glass, Anne answered Elizabeth, "Good. We had a few scares though. First, there was Nicholas falling from the tree, and then Louise's accident."

"By Louise you mean one of the Musgrove girls?" asked Mr. Elliot.

"Uh-huh," said Anne, taking another bite of her dinner.

"We got your email about Nick. How's my grandson, the little bugger, doing?" Mr. Elliot passed his bowl to Susan for seconds, enjoying the delicious food.

"Much better," Anne answered.

"Good...good..." He rubbed his hands together, anticipating the warm and succulent flavors in his mouth.

"So, what was the event at the country club?" Anne asked Elizabeth.

"You remember Will Elliot don't you? My old boyfriend from school? Well, he invited us to play tennis. He's very good. In fact, he almost went pro back in college."

Anne was taken aback. Here she'd assumed the "event" was relaxing body treatments! Good thing she never gambled! But what surprised Anne the most was hearing the name of Will Elliot again. Anne uttered her amazement, "Will Elliot? I thought..."

Elizabeth interrupted her in a curt manner, "That was a long time ago, Anne. Dad and I decided to let bygones be bygones."

Anne could tell from Elizabeth's response her sister was annoyed and wanted no further probing. Even so, Anne's curiosity wanted more answers. "But isn't he still married?"

Susan, at seeing the look of irritation on Elizabeth's face, answered on her friend's behalf, "No, I understand his wife died a year ago."

"Well, it could be just a coincidence," Anne stated, "But when Mary and I were at a restaurant in Lincoln City, they paged a man with the same name. When did you say he arrived in Napa Valley?"

"Actually, I didn't mention it," Elizabeth said snidely, ripping off a piece of bread and stuffing it in her mouth. Anne was surprised at her sister's reaction. *Why is Elizabeth being so nasty?* she thought. It was obvious that negative vibes were being aimed directly towards her from Elizabeth. *Could she be feeling threatened? Of me?*

"Will arrived about four days ago," Mr. Elliot said, answering in place of Elizabeth. "He heard we were in town and decided to give us a call hoping we might join him for dinner. Fine young man if you ask me."

Elizabeth smiled, pleased at her father's comment regarding Will, then picking up her plate, added, "Dad invited him over for lunch this Saturday." Elizabeth disappeared into the kitchen, but her voice was still audible. "I was thinking you could make that cold pasta dish we all like."

Before Anne could respond, Mr. Elliot addressed her with excitement, "Speaking of seeing people, you'll never guess who I heard from! My cousin, Missy Dee! She's here in the area for a movie premiere."

"Really?" Anne replied somewhat curiously. She had often heard her father speak of their family's highly famous cousin but had yet to meet her.

This revelation however was even bigger news to Susan, who exclaimed with animation, "My goodness! You're related to her! I've seen quite a number of her films. She's amazing! How I'd love to meet her."

Mr. Elliot was delighted at Susan's response. "Well dear, then you shall." Susan beamed as he patted her hand affectionately and showed obvious pleasure at her appropriate reaction.

It wasn't that Anne didn't like Susan, but she just didn't trust her. As Anne now observed the closeness that had grown between her father and Susan over the past few months, her brow creased with worry. She knew Susan's past and couldn't easily forget the time Elizabeth's friend had hung on the arm of an ancient-looking man at a charity function her family attended a few years ago. Susan had bamboozled the foolish old geezer, even managing to flatter him all the way to the altar. But when the money ran out, Susan deserted him without any sign of remorse. Anne didn't care to have her father be Susan's next victim.

Chapter 30

Mr. Elliot had arranged for the four of them to meet Missy Dee later that week at Dietros, an upscale café in downtown Sacramento. Because of Missy Dee's celebrity status, they were given red-carpet treatment and the food was ready in record time. However, actually getting to *enjoy* the tasty items was a different matter all together. Everyone felt on edge as they attempted to eat delicately while under the microscope of a dozen or so camera lenses. Photographers had been hounding the establishment since their arrival, trying to get some front page photographic material of the newsworthy star.

Missy toyed with the food on her plate while feigning an appreciation for her lunch companions. Studying Missy, Anne found the star's appearance quite ridiculous. Missy was wearing big dark sunglasses and had her hair cut in a lop-sided bob that would have looked silly on anyone but a movie star. Not only that, Missy's manner of dress was unique to say the very least. Anne was almost embarrassed to be seen with her. Unlike most people, Anne did not have the disposition to be star struck over celebrities. Rather, she preferred to base her friendships and devotion on those who had integrity, compassion, and humility. So far, Anne had not seen much, if any, of those character traits in Missy Dee.

"Stupid paparazzi, always following me around," Missy murmured through her teeth as she posed a few times, smiling. "I never get a moment's peace."

Anne inwardly cringed as she watched Susan use an opportune break in the conversation to butter up Missy Dee. "You were brilliant in *Let Me Go*," Susan began, "That scene where you hyperventilated, how did you ever do it?"

Missy glanced sideways at her and answered in a condescending tone, "It's my job." Before Susan could fawn further over the star, Missy unexpectedly motioned a waitress to their table, "Excuse me," her voice rang out demandingly.

Anne wondered what it was that Missy could want. The awestruck waitress excitedly hurried over to them, glad for an opportunity to be noticed by such a famous actress.

Provoking Anne to sheer wonderment, she watched as Missy lifted up the bread from her sandwich for the waitress to see inside. "Is that mayo? *I think* it's mayo. What does Missy not like on her sandwiches? Mayo."

"I am so sorry, Missy," the waitress began apologizing, "I'll get you another sandwich right away."

Before the waitress could remove the offending item, Missy shocked everyone by throwing the slice with mayo onto the ground. Anne was speechless. She glanced around to notice that most everyone in the restaurant had witnessed the entire scene. Anne sat there awkwardly, observing the unnatural hush that had come over the previously noisy and bustling café. The only things still moving were the photographers who snapped hungrily at the slab of juicy coverage Missy had just thrown their way.

With flaming cheeks, the waitress hurriedly kneeled to pick up the piece of bread, but the imprint of the mayo remained on the ground. As the waitress reached for a cloth to remove the gooey substance from the floor, Anne watched in what seemed like slow motion as Missy flung the remaining sandwich at the clueless young woman. Anne was horrified! The poor waitress' lips quivered as she touched the mustard and bits of lettuce which now streaked her once clean hair. Scrambling up quickly, the humiliated girl left the table in tears. Anne started to go after the waitress to apologize, but her father restrained her by placing a hand on her arm along with a warning look. Anne froze in her place, having to suffer while watching Missy stick her nose in the air as if *she* had been the offended victim.

"Stupid girl," Missy hissed obnoxiously while pulling out her iPhone to compose a text. "Such incompetence," she added with contempt. Missy purposely began to raise her voice to get the attention of the other staff and patrons. "These people better not be expecting a tip." Then pausing for a second, she let out a crude laugh, "Although I will 'tip' my friends never to eat here." Missy appeared quite pleased at her play on words, but Anne only felt disgust at this cruel, egotistical woman.

Anne felt paralyzed to improve the situation with her father keeping her in check. When a different waitress appeared, Anne felt like sinking under the café's table— *What else will Missy do to worsen the situation?* she thought in bewilderment.

The waitress placed a new sandwich in front of Missy and scurried away.

"And by the way," Missy called after her, "I'm not paying for this," she stated before sinking her teeth into the quality sandwich. The waitress looked over at her manager, who reluctantly nodded his approval. "What a dreadful place," continued Missy between mouthfuls of her lunch. Anne mused that for being such a "dreadful" place, Missy must be finding the food quite delicious judging by how quickly she was devouring it.

Anne stared at the star with disbelief, taking note of Missy Dee's prima donna attitude and wished she were anywhere but in the company of her cousin. With disgust, Anne surmised Missy most likely made the scene just so she could get a free sandwich. *Is my family so blinded by Missy Dee's celebrity sta-*

tus that they can't see how unacceptable her behavior is? Although Anne now realized it was probably wise of her father to have stopped her from going after the waitress, since it would have only provided additional fodder for the paparazzi, but why hadn't he reprimanded Missy in private for acting so wrong?

As Missy Dee led her family out of the restaurant, Anne lingered to apologize to the staff and made sure they were compensated for Missy's meal. Although the manager at first refused, he finally accepted the money along with her deepest apologies. Her family may have tolerated such poor behavior, but Anne would not. What Missy did was wrong, and Anne did her best to make it right.

Chapter 31

"So, how do you like the new place?" Carol asked Anne the next day. Carol was waiting in line at Starbucks and had decided to give Anne a call to see how the move to Sacramento had gone.

Unlike Carol, Anne was working off her earlier Starbuck caloric intake by speed walking through the new neighborhood. Anne reflected on how refreshing it was to talk with Carol in comparison to the daily interactions with her family, or the humiliating ordeal with Missy the day before. Carol actually cared, and that in itself made a world of a difference. Smiling, Anne surveyed the expensive homes flocking the California hillside and replied, "It's surprisingly very nice."

Carol seemed disappointed and sighed, inhaling the pungent smell of roasted coffee beans. Moving up another spot in line, she answered, "I was hoping you'd hate it. It's going to be so different not having you here," she pouted. Finally reaching the counter, the cashier began impatiently tapping a foot while waiting for Carol to order. Sensing the annoyed stares from behind, Carol added, "Just a second, Anne—" Lowering the phone, she quickly scanned the menu and decided to select her daily favorite. "I'll have a tall, nonfat, peppermint mocha."

The cashier wrote the order on a cup. "That will be $3.65."

Carol swiped her debit card and punched in her PIN number. "Sorry about that," she resumed, able to talk again now that her transaction was complete.

"That's okay," Anne answered in between breaths as she scaled a steep hill.

"Did I mention that I'll be in California next week?" The barista called out Carol's order and she promptly stepped forward to claim the steaming beverage. "It's for business, but…"

"That's wonderful!" Anne interrupted her, "Although we don't have room in the house, what with us downsizing and all, I'm hoping you'll still come and visit me?"

Carol sounded pleased. "Good—that's what I was hoping you'd say."

"Really, Carol! You know you never have to fish for an invite! After all, you're like a second mom to me."

Carol smiled with genuine pleasure as she pushed the glass doors open and exited Starbucks, beginning to walk the streets in downtown Portland. "That touches me to hear you say that, Anne."

"Good!" Anne said, then with a mischievous tone in her voice added, "Does that mean I can borrow your Gucci bag?"

"I'm not *that* touched!" Carol laughed, pausing to take a drink of her warm mocha. "No, seriously, Anne, it does really mean a lot. Ever since your mother died, I've tried to council you the way I believe she would have. Emma was my dearest friend…" Carol slowed her pace, nostalgically remembering Anne's mom, Carol's true kindred spirit.

Anne slowed her pace as well, almost to a standstill. Taking a deep breath, she closed her eyes. "I know…I miss her, too."

Chapter 32

The next day, Anne found herself finishing the final preparations for lunch while Elizabeth stood nearby, gazing out the kitchen window. Her sister was eagerly awaiting the arrival of the notorious Will Elliot, who was to grace them with his presence that afternoon. The whole house had been in a buzz that morning with the expectation of his arrival. Elizabeth had spent hours perfecting her hair and makeup, and it showed. She looked exquisite.

Anne hadn't seen her sister get this excited about a guy since…well…actually never. Now observing Elizabeth twiddle her thumbs while in wait for the man who had caused so much drama in years past, Anne was curious at what special qualities this Will possessed to so thoroughly bewitch her sister.

Breaking away from this musing, Anne caught Elizabeth attempting to snatch a piece of the sourdough bread which Anne had made. As she playfully tapped Elizabeth's hand, her sister looked offended.

"Ouch!" Elizabeth said, highly overreacting. Despite the "painful" slap, Elizabeth still managed to put the pilfered morsel into her mouth. Before Anne could object further, Elizabeth interrupted excitedly with a shrill voice, "There he is!"

Startled, Anne stepped back as Elizabeth nearly knocked her down to scurry to a small mirror to primp her hair.

Once Anne's ears had stopped ringing from the triumphant announcement heralding Will's arrival, she peered out the window above the sink hoping to catch a glimpse of their guest. Instead, the only thing in view was a red Corvette parked in their driveway. *Figures*, Anne thought with a sigh, *Any man Elizabeth finds attractive has to drive a fancy car.*

"Dad! Susan! Will's here!" Elizabeth shouted with glee just as they heard the doorbell ring. Taking one last look at herself in the mirror, Elizabeth rushed to answer it.

"Hi, Will! Come on in," Anne heard Elizabeth say in her most charming voice. Anne continued to listen as Elizabeth ushered him into the living room where their dad and Susan were sitting.

Being curious to find out if the "Will" currently in their home was the same stranger from the beach, Anne plucked up the courage to check things out for herself. Entering the room, Anne was glad to discover that Will was not facing her as it allowed her to scope him out momentarily, albeit from the back. Even from that angle, Anne recognized him as the man from Lincoln City.

"Oh, there she is!" Mr. Elliot called out, drawing all attention to Anne. "I don't believe you've ever met my daughter Anne," he said as he motioned Will in her direction.

Will turned with a ready smile only to give a double take, indicating his recognition of her. Seeing the rather goofy and bewildered look on his face, Anne was thankful to have had the prior knowledge so her face did not mirror his surprised reaction. But even with the silly expression on Will's face, Anne had to admit he was extremely handsome. Forcing herself to suppress a giggle, she held out her hand in greeting to welcome him with a dazzling smile. Will quickly exchanged the initial look of shock to one of pleasure.

"No, but...ahh," Will answered her father mischievously, taking hold of Anne's hand. "We actually saw each other at Lincoln City, didn't we?"

Anne smiled, "Dear Watson, I do believe you're right."

Will was, in any girl's book, a hunk. He was of nice height, well-built, and had a chiseled face that belonged on the cover of *GQ*. In fact, Anne now recalled Elizabeth mentioning previously that Will had done some modeling in the past.

"Will," Elizabeth interjected in a voice that showed her threatened state, "Please, have a seat next to me." She patted the chair next to her and he obliged. Feeling more confident with Will now at her side, Elizabeth began to extol on his accomplishments. "Anne," she said, "You do know that Will is a host for an MTV show?" Before Anne could reply, a spiteful gleam shone in Elizabeth's eyes as she added, "Oh, I forgot," she continued with malice, "You don't care about stuff like that." Elizabeth shot Anne a back-off look, causing Will to glance curiously between the two sisters.

Anne took a deep breath and tried to pretend her sister wasn't turning this introduction into a drama scene. "Actually, I didn't know, but that doesn't mean I don't care. In fact," she said, turning to Will, "I find it quite fascinating. How did you ever land a job like that?" Anne asked.

Will looked pleased at her interest, "I was a contestant on another MTV reality show called *The Real World* a few years back. I guess I generated enough of a following that they offered me my current gig."

Although Anne wasn't a fan of MTV or the show *The Real World*, she had to give Will props for achieving what must be a very lucrative job.

Her father, growing hungry, spoke up, "Anne made us lunch. She's quite the accomplished cook," he added, obtuse to the climate in the room.

Oh, why did Dad have to brag about my cooking? Anne thought, *Talk about putting pressure on my culinary skills!* She just prayed that all of her food selections would turn out to be edible.

"Really?" Will studied her with a new look of esteem.

Anne smiled shyly, "Well, let's hope I can live up to my dad's appreciation of my cooking."

"I doubt you'd present anything I wouldn't want," Will said with a admiring glint in his eyes. For some reason, the look made Anne rather uncomfortable.

In an effort to escape his forward eyes, Anne invited everyone into the dining room to start them on appetizers while she finalized what hopefully would be a tasty lunch.

The table Anne set was elegant. She had spied some beautiful flowers in the backyard greenhouse and decided to use them as a centerpiece. Along with the "cold pasta dish" her sister had requested for lunch (which was actually a chilled Chicken Basil Linguini), Anne had prepared a fruit salad and homemade sourdough bread. It was a light meal, but purposely so—for dessert was "Death by Chocolate".

To Anne's confusion, and Elizabeth's dismay, all through lunch, Will seemed more intent on conversing with Anne. To make matters worse, Elizabeth was becoming quite jealous and downright mean with every observation of Will's marked admiration of her sister.

At first, Elizabeth assumed it was a tactic by Will to make her jealous—perhaps he thought it would make him more in demand. If so, Will was completely off base—all it did was provoke intense anger. What frustrated Elizabeth the most was knowing she was considered the beauty, so why did Will wish to spend so much time gawking at Anne, who in her eyes, was quite plain? And why would Will exert such effort to change the seating assignments so as to sit next to her sister? Elizabeth simply couldn't comprehend it.

Hoping to find some sympathy from Susan, Elizabeth attempted to secure her friend's attention, but Susan was too occupied doting on her father. Resigning herself to seclusion, Elizabeth sunk into her chair and began to give Anne the evil eye while playing idly with her food.

Anne, on the other hand, was finding herself attracted to Will's personality despite her initial misgivings. Will was actually quite funny, and surprisingly knew endless bits of trivia which Anne found fascinating. With each passing moment, she was becoming more intrigued by Will but knew she needed to remain cautious in her admiration. After all, a guy that good looking couldn't be trusted, right?

As dinner was wrapping up, Susan elected to share the recent story of Missy Dee, recounting in vivid detail the incident of the infamous sandwich. Will found the story entertaining, and while helping to clear the table, he continued to speak to Anne of Missy Dee.

"It sounds like your visit with your cousin was quite memorable to say the least," he said with a slight smirk.

Anne headed towards the kitchen with Will following her. "You can say that again!" she rolled her eyes playfully, "Most movie stars today think they are practically little gods. I'm sorry to say Missy's not what I categorize as good company."

With an inquisitive smile, Will prompted, "Okay, now I'm curious. What *do* you consider good company?"

By now, Anne and Will had deposited all the dishes in the sink. Anne turned around and rested her back against the base of the countertop, looking squarely at him. "My idea of good company is to spend time with people who are caring, compassionate, and intelligent. People who can exchange more than ten words in a conversation without everything pertaining to themselves." Anne paused, perplexed by Will's captivated look. He started to grin, and Anne gave him a questioning smile while finishing her statement with, "Well, anyway, that's my definition of good company."

"You're wrong," Will said, much to the surprise of Anne as he took a step towards her. "That's not *good* company...it's the best."

Anne smiled as their eyes locked for just a moment. The connection was so quick and clear, but it seemed to last forever. It was then that Anne began to feel perhaps Will was more than just a pretty face or a charmer, but actually a person whom she could relate to. She couldn't help but gaze back into his handsome eyes. They riveted her attention as if being pulled by a tractor beam. Her father's entry into the kitchen broke the enchanting atmosphere.

"Anne, we're ready for the dessert," her father said, not sensing any of the awkwardness caused by his entrance.

She slowly nodded, trying to avoid Will's eyes while reaching for the cake platter to remove the glass lid. Grabbing a knife to slice the cake, Will was beside her before she knew it.

"Nonetheless," he began, "It is important to be seen with influential people. It never does any harm being related to someone famous."

This observation by Will disappointed Anne, and she said so. "I don't care too much for acquaintances or distant family members you only keep because of their status or monetary value." Slicing the cake with a little too much enthusiasm, Anne didn't bother trying to hide that her feathers had been ruffled. Social status had always been a sensitive topic, especially after the ordeal with Rick. "Can you grab those plates in the cupboard above?" she asked, motioning to the dishes on the second shelf.

Will, realizing his faux pas, tried to smooth over the situation while retrieving the dishes. "Let's just put it this way," he said to Anne after she had served up the cake. "Maybe it's a good thing your dad has people like Missy Dee to distract him from...should we say, less advantageous acquaintances?" By the time he finished this statement they had reached the dining room and Will inclined his head with a pointed look in Susan's direction. Anne paused and looked at Will curiously, following his gaze to where Elizabeth's friend was currently making a fuss over her father.

Will licked off some of the frosting which had found its way onto his hand, "Yum...I can see where this dessert gets its name. This is positively to *die* for."

Disconcerted, Anne distributed the desserts while Will sat down to devour the chocolatety treat. Taking her place next to him, Anne decided to let the subject drop, yet still wondered about Will's interest in her father's affairs. *I too, have always suspected Susan's motives, but this should be of no concern to Will.* Anne wished she knew why her father's romantic affairs seemed to be of importance to him.

Chapter 33

Anne flipped through her iPod as she waited for Carol at the lower level luggage claim area. The flight had earlier been delayed, and now Anne was scanning the crowd for her friend. So far, all she could see were uptight passengers and airport security guards, none of whom seemed too friendly.

"Anne!"

Anne heard her name and turned to see Carol rushing towards her with arms opened wide. Instantly, a lump formed in Anne's throat. The sight of Carol always impacted her; it was like seeing her mother. Anne swiftly closed the distance between them and accepted Carol's warm embrace.

"Oh, how I've missed you!" Carol exclaimed.

"Me too!" Anne reciprocated, then pulled away to note the medium sized carry-on which now rested at their feet. "How many pieces of luggage did you bring this visit?" she asked with a mischievous look.

The last time the two of them traveled together for a girl's weekend, Carol had packed six suitcases. It had been a running joke between them ever since.

"Only three," Carol replied with mock righteousness.

Anne laughed. "I have a feeling we're going to need a forklift then."

"Really, Anne. I'm not that bad, am I?" Carol said, feigning innocence.

Spotting one of her suitcases beginning its way down the conveyor belt, Carol moved swiftly to retrieve it with Anne assisting. Exerting all of their strength to yank it off, Carol turned to Anne in triumph. "One down, two to go! Where are you parked?"

"I got lucky and found a space close to the elevator on level three," Anne answered, taking command of the suitcase for Carol.

Carol smiled in relief. "Thank goodness—my puppies are exhausted!"

Forty minutes later the two of them were on the freeway heading towards Carol's hotel.

"What a nice car! Is it yours?" Carol inquired as she took in the fine leather and smooth ride of the glitzy Mercedes.

"It's Elizabeth's," Anne answered, signaling for a lane change. "She's letting me use it until my 'junker' arrives."

"Wow, that doesn't sound characteristic of her," Carol said, shifting in her seat to get a better look at Anne.

"It isn't," Anne chuckled. "Actually Elizabeth doesn't want this car anymore. She ordered a new one which won't arrive for another week. When it does, she'll trade this one in."

"Hmm...to coin Paul Harvey, 'Now we know the rest of the story,'" Carol said, digesting the news. "Which reminds me...how about filling me in on Will Elliot? I remember meeting him once when your father and I visited Elizabeth at Dartmouth. However, after their breakup, I seem to recall your family was not on the best of terms with him. Does that mean everything is all patched up now?"

"Yes, surprisingly. Dad's now accepting him with open arms."

"Is he still as handsome?"

"Yes, very," Anne chuckled again.

"So, what do you think?" Carol inquired with a twinkle in her eye.

"Will's very nice and I like him, but I'm not sure I see us together."

Carol stared at her with a mixture of disbelief and amazement. "Really?"

Anne was a little irritated by Carol's response. Was it so odd that she wasn't madly in love with Will when he was practically still a stranger?

"I need more information, dear," Carol said, egging her on.

"I don't know," began Anne, trying hard to be careful with her words. "Maybe I just think it's weird that after all these years he's coming around again."

"Perhaps he's beginning to value the meaning of close friends and family. Regardless, if Will seems interested in you, why hesitate? You've got to admit he's rich, and considered quite a catch."

Anne looked over at Carol and rolled her eyes. "For one thing, Elizabeth still likes him. I can tell because she takes forever getting ready anytime she knows he'll be around."

"You could look really nice, too, if you wanted." Anne sent Carol a doubtful look. "Well, you could!" Carol began defending her statement, "Not that you aren't nice looking now. But why settle for nice-looking when you could be all-out amazing!"

Anne laughed, "And how is this transformation supposed to come about?" Anne was convinced her glory days were over and done with.

Carol didn't miss a beat in responding, "I'm glad you asked. I was thinking a cute haircut…some new makeup and an updated wardrobe. Don't you think it's about time you spend as much effort on yourself as you do with your greeting cards?"

Anne had a feeling Carol's speech had been rehearsed. Looking at herself in the rear-view mirror, she wondered if once again Carol was right, and perhaps it was time for a change.

Chapter 34

Four days later, Anne found herself sitting nervously in Elizabeth's Mercedes outside a popular Los Angeles shopping center. Carol had managed to secure Anne an appointment with one of the best reputed hair salons in the city, thanks to Missy Dee. When Anne considered the source of the recommendation though, it didn't give her much confidence. Instead of being pleased, Anne refused to budge from the car.

"After all the strings your cousin Missy Dee pulled to get you into the hottest salon in town, you, young lady..." Carol scolded, "...are going to keep the appointment and at least have the courtesy to hear what the stylist has to say."

Somehow, Carol managed to persuade Anne to leave the safe haven of the car to venture inside Hair Extraordinaire. Once indoors, Carol triumphantly informed the receptionist of their arrival. Soon after, the two were escorted to a stylish hair station loaded with the latest magazines containing popular hair styles. Also of interest were advertisements for hot new hair dyes, showing colors which ranged from normal to downright bizarre. Anne felt herself becoming hesitant again. After all, a dye job was nothing to sneeze at, and Anne was not one to do anything drastic.

Carol did her best to calm Anne's trepidation, extolling all the praise she'd heard regarding the stylist. Anne became bolstered by the artist's reputation, and her confidence once again soared until she laid eyes on Roberto.

Wearing what looked like a psychedelic ice-skating outfit from the 70's and having up swept hair similar to the Joker of Batman fame, Roberto sashayed his way towards Anne. He looked like a man on a mission, carefully circling her at least three times, tsk-tsking each time he passed by Anne's wary face. *So much for this being a boost to my morale,* Anne mused glumly.

At last, Roberto spoke. He was adamant Anne was in desperate need of a new hair color. Anne found him to be quite persuasive and soon Roberto's enthusiasm started to win her over. She began envisioning a new "Anne" with perhaps a darker, richer brown hue or maybe even a sprinkling of blond highlights.

Roberto leaned closer to Anne so that they were cheek to cheek gazing into the mirror. Anne froze at his invasion of her personal space. His breath reeked of anchovies—something which had never been a favorite of Anne's. Trying her best not to inhale, Anne was relieved when Roberto abruptly stood straight up to speak into an intercom for his assistant Lou Lou to come forth.

Within seconds, the helper arrived, startling them when she spoke from out of nowhere, "You know it sometimes takes Roberto a while for inspiration to hit." His assistant looked in awe at the stylist as she offered this bit of information. "But when it does," she continued, "You can be assured that it will be something out of this world! Look what he did for me!" Roberto flashed his assistant a look of pleased satisfaction as the girl now began to twirl in front of them in order to show off his workmanship.

Both Carol and Anne quickly assessed Lou Lou's hair with horror. Long hair could be seen on the girl's left side with bold blue stripes graduating to carrot orange at the top. As Lou Lou finished twirling though, they were astounded to see the assistant was completely shaved on the right side!

"I'm thinking..." began Roberto dramatically, causing silence to ensue. "Flaming red!" he declared cockily, nodding his head with satisfaction.

Anne looked frightened. "Red?" she squeaked out.

"Yes, and not just any red," he said about two inches from Anne's face, causing her to get a mouthful of his disturbing breath. "I want you to stop traffic, so it's got to be stop-sign red! The highlights will be white, and I will cut cute, chunky layers up to...here," he motioned to Anne's jaw line.

Roberto looked pleased that Anne appeared speechless—not that she wasn't, but at the moment it was his breath that was overpowering her. Anne felt like a prisoner of war, watching helplessly as Roberto started embellishing to his assistant all the supplies he needed in order to accomplish his vision for Anne's brilliant new look.

Desperate, Anne mouthed *Help*! to Carol through the mirror.

Carol, also in shock, wisely acknowledged Anne's SOS call and plucked up her courage to say something to the overly enthusiastic hair stylist. "Ah, hmm...Roberto..." she began hesitantly, "I think Anne is picturing something more...ah... subtle."

Roberto wheeled around to look at Carol, his face a mixture of injured pride and anger at his genius being questioned. His assistant looked aghast and stepped towards him protectively, placing a hand on his shoulder to show Roberto she still believed in him.

"You do not like my ideas?" he huffed.

Carol tried to soothe him, although there really was no way of beating around the bush. "Oh...it's not that, it's just... Anne's a little old-fashioned."

Roberto lowered his eyes and nodded. "Fine...I don't work with people who don't trust me." With that, he raised his hands in surrender and walked away with a dejected air.

Bewildered, Anne looked to Carol for confirmation that this wasn't just some planned television prank. Horrific visions of herself being featured on *Candid Camera* flashed through Anne's mind.

Shrugging, Carol whispered, "Apparently, Roberto doesn't like to be questioned."

His assistant who remained shook her head disapprovingly at Carol's comment. "He's a genius! Only a fool dares to go against Roberto," she declared, her voice a mixture of utter contempt and admonishment.

"Lou Lou!" Roberto called from across the parlor, sparing them from further chastisement by the assistant who eagerly turned to see what Roberto wanted.

What Carol and Anne observed next made the whole situation seem even more surreal. Roberto was clearly sulking, having seated himself in what could only be described as a king's throne. The ornate piece of furniture was about six feet tall with plush velvet fabric and costumed beading set in the elaborately carved wood.

Roberto's assistant hurried anxiously to him, begging to know what she could do to comfort him.

"You've got to be kidding me," Carol said with disbelief, looking towards Anne who could only suppress a smirk. Carol nudged Anne, "Girl, you owe me big time for saving you!"

"I don't see where I owe you anything," hissed Anne in a whispered breath, "I didn't even want to come here in the first place!"

"In that case," taunted Carol, "Perhaps I should get Roberto's attention and tell him you've changed your mind?" She began to raise her arm in pretense to catch Roberto's eye.

Anne panicked and held Carol in check, "Okay, okay, I owe you! Just save me from being a flaming stop sign with a crew cut!"

Lou Lou's voice cut through the salon, "Quick, get me a paper sack! Roberto is hyperventilating!" Anne and Carol turned simultaneously to observe his frantic assistant trying her best to calm the distraught Roberto.

"Oh dear! I feel terrible!" Anne exclaimed.

"Bad enough to let him have his way?" teased Carol.

Anne reared her head up quickly, "Not that bad!"

A sack was brought pronto to the distraught stylist, and soon Roberto began to settle down once realizing he was once again the center of attention. He even dared to hope that all the hoopla might cause Anne to relent and beg him to do her hair after all. Unfortunately for Roberto, this was something Anne would never do in a million years. As if sensing Anne's thoughts, Lou Lou sent a mean stare in their direction.

Anne tugged on Carol's hand, "Let's get out of here quick before Lou Lou comes back or an ambulance arrives."

Carol didn't have to be asked twice. Grabbing their bags, they bolted through the front doors, managing to suppress their laughter until out of earshot.

Once safely in their vehicle, Carol relaxed in her seat and sighed, "I hope the salon doesn't hold us responsible for any counseling Roberto will need."

Anne shook her head and looked to the ceiling. "Hairstylists," she said with mock exasperation.

Chapter 35

Early Monday morning, Anne was once again sitting in a styling chair, but this time at an Aveda Salon. Her hair had been washed, cut, and was now covered in layers of foil while the two selected hair colors set in. Carol wouldn't stop at these few changes either: once Anne's hair was complete, Carol had arranged for the salon's makeup artist to give Anne a complete new look, including a facial.

Despite Anne's initial misgivings, she found herself getting excited to see the finished outcome. Nearly three hours later, after all tasks were done, Anne studied herself in the mirror and had to admit she was pleased. She barely recognized the radiant woman staring back at her in the mirror. Her once single-length long hair was now layered, starting at her shoulders. The colorist had added deep mahogany highlights to Anne's hair which added a beautiful sheen. Her locks felt so light and silky. Anne made the salon team laugh as she swung her hair about as if she was in a hair product commercial.

As to her makeup, the artist showed Anne how to accentuate her eyes without making it appear as though she was wearing tons of makeup. That pleased Anne, as she preferred a more natural look. Anne liked how feminine she felt, and wondered why she had stopped doing the little things that made her proud to be a woman—like taking the extra time to style her hair long rather than scooping it into a ponytail, or accentuating her eyes to make them stand out. She felt empowered and didn't want the day to end, so when Carol suggested the two enjoy lunch together and then afterwards hit the stores, Anne didn't have to think twice.

Carol felt quite smug when she noticed Anne catching the attention of several guys in the restaurant as the duo made their way to the table. After all, it was Carol who was the instigator of this beauty transformation.

"Anne, you look years younger," Carol said when perusing the menu a moment later. "We must find clothes to match your new look!"

Anne nodded excitedly, blushing at the admiring eyes watching her from the various tables around the establishment. It felt good to be noticed. Especially after the bruising comment made by Rick to Mary about how he'd barely recognized her.

Ordering a Caesar salad and a cup of soup, Anne refreshed herself. She needed to gear up for what would likely be a long session of shopping therapy with "Dr." Carol.

Seven full shopping bags later, Anne collapsed into the driver's seat beside Carol. Anne needed a breather before taking on the evening's California traffic.

"I had a great time today, Anne," Carol looked over to smile sweetly at her god-daughter.

"Me, too," Anne smiled back. "Thanks for setting everything up. I really needed this."

Carol placed her hand on Anne's arm, "I know."

Anne felt the tears sting her eyes, but kept them in check. "Time to hit the road?" she asked. Carol nodded and Anne started the engine.

After Anne dropped Carol off at her hotel, she made her way back home wondering if her family would notice the change in her appearance. As she came in the front door, Anne could see her father attempting to arrange his tie in the hallway mirror. Her mother had always taken care of this task for her husband, and even though it'd been years since Emma's passing, her father had yet to master this art.

Hearing Anne enter, her dad glanced over, quickly doing a double take. Turning to give his full admiration, he smiled. "My, my...you're looking very nice."

Anne put down her purse and shopping bags, reveling for once that her father was actually pleased to see her. Surprisingly, she now felt shy and tucked one foot behind the other, unsure of how to reply.

Walter was about to say more, but Elizabeth's voice interrupted him. "Dad, I hope you're just about ready. We'll need to leave in five minutes or we'll be late," she commanded from the upstairs hallway.

Refocusing his efforts to the untied tie, Walter turned his attention back to the mirror and continued to fidget with it. Anne sighed, sorry that the moment had been lost but seeing her dad needed help, chose to assist him.

"Where are you going?" she asked as he lowered his hands in surrender, allowing Anne to work her magic. She had memorized the intricate folds her mother used all those years ago.

"Didn't you get my call earlier?" her father said with exasperation. Before Anne could answer, he explained, "Missy invited us to attend the premiere showing of her new movie. You're to come too, so you'd better hurry. Missy doesn't like to wait."

"Sorry, I won't be able to go. I'm meeting my former school teacher," Anne said matter-of-factly as she artfully applied the finishing tugs to his tie.

Perturbed at this news, Walter checked the finished product in the mirror. Anne could tell by his expression that he wasn't going to let her refusal drop. He wanted her there, and couldn't understand why Anne would stick with her prior plans when a celebrity movie premiere was dangling within her grasp.

Turning to his daughter with exasperation, he put his hands on Anne's arms. "Come now, we are talking Missy Dee here! You don't know how fortunate you are to be related to her. Can't you see whoever this person is tomorrow?" Hearing Elizabeth's footsteps on the stairs, Walter grabbed his dinner jacket and began to pull it on. "Who is it anyway? Do I know them?" her father asked, his voice rankled with irritation.

"Her name is Mrs. Smith, and I don't think so, since you never came to any of my school functions." Anne didn't bother looking up to observe her dad's expression at this cutting comment. "I've already committed myself and don't want to disappoint her," she finished, Anne's tone expressing her unwavering stance.

"How important could this person be in comparison to Missy?" Mr. Elliot whined. "I can't believe you'd rather see some boring, old school teacher named 'Mrs. Smith'—a *nobody*—than to hob-knob with celebrities!" Her father's voice rose along with his disbelief.

Anne didn't care for her dad's prejudice, nor did she think it was kind to trivialize and demean her kind-hearted teacher. Unwilling to back down, Anne began defending her decision. "First off, she's not boring, and as far as—"

"Dad!" Elizabeth chastised as she entered the foyer, interrupting Anne. "Please! Can't you play catch-up some other time?!"

As her sister turned the corner, she came in view of Anne and noticed the new look. Elizabeth's expression showed she did not share in her father's approval of Anne's transformation. "Well, well. It's been a while since you took such pains with your appearance. Are you sure it's not a 'Mister' Smith you're meeting?" she asked snidely.

Anne was about to object when her father cut in sternly, "Anne's not one to lie, Elizabeth."

Elizabeth rolled her eyes with frustration, pointing to the clock. "Um, Dad, we need to leave now!"

Not bothering to wait for a response, Elizabeth stormed out of the house. Walter studied Anne for a moment, almost as if attempting to see if there was truly any Elliot blood inside of her. Anne looked away, feeling like the black sheep of the family. She knew she'd never quite fit in, but still, Anne had always sought her father's approval regardless of the outcome. To Anne's ongoing disappointment, her dad sent one more disapproving look in her direction before leaving. Anne was left by herself in the empty room, reflecting how just fifteen minutes earlier she had been happy and feeling confident—but now Anne felt alone and wanted to cry. She hoped that a dose of her old school teacher would be the cure to turn things around.

Chapter 36

"Anne!" Jane Smith exclaimed, beaming with delight from her bed at seeing Anne enter the dimly-lit assisted-living apartment.

Anne was touched by the warm greeting, and secretly, it was all that she'd hoped for. Jane had always been a bright spot in her past, having taken Anne under her wing during some of the most difficult trials in her life.

Jane's caregiver was combing the patient's hair and greeted her charge's guest with a friendly grin. Anne smiled at both, but with tenderness towards Jane as she moved to her side, sitting in the empty chair next to the bed.

Jane Smith had been such an encouragement and mentor to Anne after her mother's death. This dear teacher knew firsthand what it meant to lose a parent. Jane also had experienced the loss of her own mother at a young age and was able to recognize the emptiness and fear in Anne. The two had remained close since Anne's sophomore year at high school.

"Oh, Anne! I am so happy to see you!" continued Mrs. Smith, tenderly stroking Anne's cheek with her weathered hand. "Look at you! You're so beautiful!"

Anne smiled kindly, blushing as she did so. She took Jane's hand and held it in her own. "And how are you?" Anne asked, "Is everything alright?"

179

The death of Jane's husband and her present sickness had taken a toll on this dear lady's appearance. Anne couldn't help but notice that Mrs. Smith had aged significantly since she'd last seen her. However, Jane's graying hair and weather-beaten skin couldn't diminish her still bright and lively eyes. The elderly lady's smile transformed her face, allowing Anne a glimpse of the woman's former beauty.

Jane shrugged her shoulders. "As well as can be expected...considering the doctor said I must stay confined to my bed. I told Nurse Rooke I feel like a hostage!" Jane winked at her caregiver and Nurse Rooke chuckled. "But then again, I couldn't get up and walk out of here even if I was allowed to," she continued. "Still, I am quite content. I won't say it doesn't become discouraging at times, but I try to always look at the positive."

Jane's eyes illuminated with an inner happiness and contentment that was hard to explain. Anne's admiration for her friend grew. She only hoped that if placed in similar circumstances, she could emit the same joy as Jane.

The old teacher squeezed Anne's hand, and then sent her a playful look. "Besides, who needs to go out and about when Nurse Rooke brings me all the entertainment I need."

"And what would that be?" Anne asked in curiosity.

"Delicious gossip!" Jane said, sharing an inside chuckle with Nurse Rooke. The two ladies' enjoyment was contagious, and Anne found herself laughing.

"Is that so? Let me guess..." Anne said, baiting them on. "...that 'Harold' in room 313 is getting a colonoscopy?"

The three of them shared another laugh, but once the merriment died down somewhat Jane answered, "Oh, you'd be surprised! In fact," Jane directed a look at Nurse Rooke conspiratorially, "How about supplying my young friend here with a little something concerning herself?"

At this announcement, Anne sat in confusion. Nurse Rooke shifted in her seat with newfound importance, "Certainly. Well, I just happen to know..." she paused for effect,

"...that a certain young man named Will Elliot thinks very highly of you," Nurse Rooke said triumphantly.

Anne stared with disbelief. They had to be joking! Since she hadn't lived in California very long, who at a hospital would be talking about her? "Where on earth did you hear that?" she asked, not sure whether to laugh or feel alarmed.

Motioning for Anne to remain calm, Nurse Rooke explained, "It's all because of my other job. You see, Mr. Wallis and Will Elliot are tennis partners."

Apparently Nurse Rooke thought this explanation to be enough, but Anne was still much in the dark. She couldn't make the connection. *How could Nurse Rooke's work be connected with that?*

Realizing the confusion, Nurse Rooke continued, "Mrs. Wallis just had a baby, and I help out with the family on Wednesdays. Anyways, Mrs. Wallis told me that Mr. Wallis said that Will said—"

"You can stop! I'm convinced!" Anne interrupted her, scrunching her face in disbelief and rolling her eyes. She glanced between the two chuckling conspirators. With both of them being so entertaining, Anne knew she was going to enjoy herself immensely the rest of the evening. Resting back into her seat, Anne was glad she had stood her ground and not been persuaded to join her family at the movie premiere. No way would she be having as much fun as this.

Chapter 37

Since settling in Napa Valley with her family, Anne had established a comfortable, if not boring routine. She filled her days mostly by working on card designs, occasional visits to the hospital to see Jane, running errands, cooking and participating in family activities. Her life wasn't exciting, but Anne was comfortable.

That particular morning she felt especially productive. Having already picked up their family's weekly groceries and returned the movie for her sister, Anne was now completing the final errand on her list. Leaving the post office with a stack of mail in her hand, Anne began to casually flip through the letters as she made her way down the sidewalk. There was one addressed to her from Mary, a couple of bills and some junk mail, but the last one caught Anne's interest. It was an envelope bearing the Hallmark crest and name. She quickly opened it. Anne had been waiting anxiously the past few weeks for a reply concerning the portfolio she submitted at their request. Anne hoped beyond hope that Hallmark deemed her designs worthy enough to bring her on board and showcase her original concepts. Anne quickly scanned the printed letter.

Dear Ms. Elliot:

After careful consideration of your submitted portfolio, Hallmark is pleased to offer you your own signature line...

Elated, Anne didn't bother reading the rest of the letter just then. Instead, she stuffed the remainder of the mail into her bag and reached for her cell phone. Anne excitedly dialed Carol's number and listened as the rings sounded. She tried to calm herself, unsure how to relate the news to Carol without first letting out an enthusiastic shriek. Carol was Anne's core supporter and firmly believed her god-daughter's work deserved recognition. Anne knew Carol would want to share in this wonderful news. After several rings though, Anne's spirits were dampened when only a voice message greeting clicked on. Ending the call, Anne sighed as she put the phone back into her purse, deciding to try again later.

A little frustrated at having to keep this exciting news to herself for the time being, Anne continued down the lonesome street, wishing she had someone to talk with. Rounding the corner to where her car was housed in a parking garage, Anne almost collided with an elderly man. To her surprise, it was Cedric Croft! Of all people, Anne would never have expected to see him, and this left her momentarily speechless. Finally, she blurted out, "Admiral Croft?"

Getting a good look at her for the first time, he cracked a smile. "Why, Anne!" he said with obvious joy at seeing her. "How are you?"

"I'm fine." Then with a giant grin she continued, "Actually, I'm better than fine. I just found out Hallmark accepted my designs for their spring collection!"

"Anne, that's wonderful!" exclaimed Admiral Croft. "I'm happy for you."

Anne could see from his demeanor that he genuinely meant it. "Thank you!" she smiled, taking his extended hand with congratulations. She silently also thanked God for providing someone to share her good news with. "What brings you to the Valley?" Anne asked, trying to connect the dots as to how he got there.

"Oh...Mrs. Croft and I desired to do some exploring in California and Rick recommended the Napa area."

"Well, I'm very glad to see you!" Anne said, readjusting her purse on her shoulder. It felt like a heavy weight now that the excitement of the Hallmark news was wearing off.

"Which way are you headed?" Cedric asked, looking in both directions to see if he had neglected any companions Anne might have with her.

"Um...this way," Anne motioned, and the two began walking together. Turning to look at the Admiral as they continued down the street, Anne asked, "Any news about Louise? Is she any better?" She had heard through Mary that Mrs. Musgrove and Mrs. Croft had become close friends through the incident.

"Oh, very much so," he answered to Anne's satisfaction, but then added, "In fact, she's gotten engaged to be married."

Anne instantly froze, fear seizing her heart.

Admiral Croft stopped in accord and looked at her oddly. "Are you okay, dear?" he asked.

Forcing her legs to move again, Anne nodded but couldn't recreate the smile which had been beaming on her face moments before. Thankfully, the Admiral didn't notice.

"If you recall, I once thought she would do well for Rick," he continued, oblivious to the change in Anne's behavior as she walked awkwardly next to him. "Well, it seems that during her recovery she and Ben fell in love instead."

Anne's throat caught. She felt like simultaneously laughing and crying as relief flooded her heart. So many thoughts raced through her mind while her face flushed and the beaming smile returned. "Engaged to Ben?" Anne asked, flabbergasted. "But they are so different!"

"Yes, but you know the old saying that opposites attract, though apparently Ben and Louise do have *one* thing in common," Cedric said with a twinkle in his eye.

Anne took the bait. "And what is that?"

"They each share a love of poetry, which probably helped to fuel the romance." Admiral Croft smiled cheekily.

"So poetry paved the way!" exclaimed Anne.

The Admiral nodded and Anne laughed, taking his proffered arm and guiding him through the parking garage's entrance.

"I would never have guessed!" she said, still quite a bit in shock.

"Me, neither," confessed the Admiral. "Rick is taking it very well though. To hear him speak, you'd never think he was interested in her romantically at all. Well, guess the poor boy will have to start all over again."

Anne pondered over the Admiral's words. *Could it be possible that Rick wasn't in love with Louise? That maybe, just maybe...his feelings for me have been reawakened?* Scoffing at herself, Anne considered how easily her imagination ran wild with silly dreams of a future existing between herself and Rick. Who was she kidding? Just because Rick didn't want Louise, didn't necessarily mean he wanted to be with her! Otherwise, why hadn't he pursued the relationship upon seeing her again—nor did it explain why Rick allowed all those years to go by without a word. *Don't be stupid!* Severely scolding herself, she pushed away these foolhardy thoughts from her mind, determined to focus on enjoying the rest of her walk with the Admiral.

Once again concentrating on the conversation at hand, Anne listened to Cedric speak of the delights he and Sophie discovered while touring the San Francisco Wharf. It was something Anne had yet to explore, even though she currently lived within a reasonable distance from this attraction. Listening to his animated descriptions of the pier and its playful seals, she understood why the Admiral had chosen the Navy as his profession—it was obvious he had a love affair with the sea.

Chapter 38

Anne really never had a choice. One moment she was sitting in the family's study, sketching some concepts for a new card line—and the next she found herself being trapped in a vehicle along with Elizabeth, Susan, and Will headed for the California coast line.

Will had engineered the whole thing by using a form of leverage akin to blackmail. He refused to go without her, and Elizabeth refused to go without him. What could Anne have done? Looking between Will's puppy dog eyes and dodging the daggers which Elizabeth was firing at her, Anne eventually surrendered to Will's relentless pestering. Thirty minutes later, she was wedged in the backseat of Elizabeth's European car sitting next to Will, wishing she had managed to contrive a legitimate reason for why she needed to spend time with Carol instead.

About half way to their destination, surprisingly her sister's new vehicle started to make some odd noises. Elizabeth jokingly tried to pass them off as Anne's rumbling stomach, but all knew they were doomed when the car came practically to a standstill on the highway. Moving at no more than 20 mph, the car had just enough power to take them to a welcoming gas station. The relief they all felt at not being honked at every few minutes was overwhelming. As Anne extricated herself from the vehicle in order to stretch her legs, Elizabeth sat back in her seat to shed a few frustrated tears.

"Elizabeth, if you want me to call Triple A, I'll do so," Anne kindly offered despite her sister's more than usual hostile attitude as of late.

However Elizabeth wouldn't allow herself to take Anne's offer. With an upturned nose, she answered, "No, I am capable of doing that myself."

Anne shrugged off the haughty tone in Elizabeth's voice and told the group she was headed inside to find a restroom. Moments later, the trio joined her in the air conditioned mini-mart, looking for some relief from the heat and their boredom.

While Anne listened to Elizabeth wrangle with the towing company over the phone, her eyes scanned the store's merchandise. The majority of items consisted of patriotic flags, t-shirts, hats and junk food. The Fourth of July was the next day, meaning the store would soon be clearancing much of the seasonal goods.

"What do you mean the tow truck can't be here for another fifty minutes?" Elizabeth growled as she peered outside to watch Will retrieve the insurance information she'd forgotten in the glove box. Turning back to face Anne and Susan, Elizabeth's appearance showed her displeasure. "Apparently every tow truck in this entire city is busy. And heaven knows when the taxi we ordered will get here. Unbelievable!"

Anne shrugged and continued down the mini-mart aisle, looking up just as Will entered the store again. His grin was a welcome sight compared to the frown clouding Elizabeth's features.

"Good news, ladies," he began, obviously pleased with himself regarding the information he was about to share. "You'll never guess who just pulled in for gas and is willing to help us out?!"

"Who?" Elizabeth demanded, not in a mood for guessing games.

"Missy Dee!" Will exclaimed, causing Elizabeth to look over at Susan with dramatic relief. "Good thing your car had the foresight to break down at the last gas station available for the next 70 miles," continued Will. "It makes for a rather popular spot."

Anne looked outside to see Missy sitting in her convertible while the attendant showed special attention due to her celebrity status.

"What a relief!" Elizabeth breathed.

"We're saved!" Susan laughed, happy to be rescued. Not only that, it provided Susan with an additional excuse to socialize with the star.

"Well, there is some bad news though," Will said, "Missy only has room for two of you."

Stunned, Elizabeth and Susan didn't move, but their expressions said it all. No way did they intend to be the ones left behind if they had any say.

Will didn't seem fazed by their reaction, having already anticipated their response. "I'll wait for the taxi and pay the attendant to handle the car," he suggested before turning to Anne and asking, "You won't mind waiting with me, will you?"

Anne, a bit surprised by Will's gentle tone nodded, thankful that a solution had been reached.

"Perfect," Elizabeth said, not waiting for a verbal reply from her sister. "Here's my Triple A card for the tow truck, plus you already have my car keys," she said, handing the membership information to Will as he rattled the keys in his pocket as confirmation.

"Do I have time to quickly use the ladies room?" Susan asked. She wanted to freshen up before hitching a ride with the celebrity—knowing the paparazzi might be snapping pictures and wanted to make sure she looked her best.

"Not a problem," answered Will. "Missy's having the attendant check her oil plus wash the windows in addition to refilling, so you've got some time. I'll come get you when she's ready to leave."

With that, Will turned and went back outside. Watching him meet up with Missy, Anne observed how quickly the star turned on the charm as the handsome Will approached her vehicle. Not a pretty sight, considering the age difference between the two. Missy was at least twenty years his senior.

Averting her eyes, Anne redirected her attention back to the magazine headlines, only to once again hear the little bells sound, indicating the door to the mini-mart had been opened. With her back to the entrance, Anne didn't bother glancing up, believing it to be Will. When he failed to approach her, Anne turned towards the door for an explanation. Her earlier assumption regarding who had entered the store couldn't have been more wrong.

With shaking legs and a flushed face, Anne found herself less than twenty feet away from the one man who occupied her every waking thought—Rick. Shocked and awed, all Anne could do was stare at him while he waited in line at the counter.

"Rick!" she said out loud unconsciously. Immediately, Anne regretted her spontaneous reaction, wishing instead she had kept silent to better compose herself. At hearing Anne's voice, Rick looked up in equal surprise.

Upon spying her, Rick's welcoming stance combined with the pleased look in his eyes was all it took for Anne to swiftly close the distance between them. Greeting him with a profuse smile, it was hard to keep her joy guarded—reminding Anne of earlier times when being happy around Rick was something that came so natural.

"I...I didn't know you were here in California," Anne stuttered out, being the first to break the silence.

"Yes. Harve and I just arrived this morning. I'm scheduled for a book signing next week but decided to come down early," Rick explained.

Not knowing what to say next, both simply stood there to gaze into each others eyes, content for the moment to search for any feelings stirring within.

"Oh...um...please say hi to Harve for me," Anne finally said, trying to think of something to bridge the silence.

"I will," he answered, her comment jarring him back to reality. "And how is your family?" Rick inquired.

"Very good," Anne answered, grateful that this time Rick broke the silence. She wished she could think of something more to say in reply, but found herself at a loss for words.

"And you? How are you doing?" Rick asked Anne pointedly.

"Better... *now*," Anne smiled. She hadn't quite meant for that to come out but maybe it was a good thing for Rick to know he still had an effect on her. Rick's quizzical look told Anne that although this revelation was a surprise to him, it was definitely a pleasant one. They remained in this fashion for another few precious seconds as if time stood still.

Susan by now had freshened up, and upon leaving the restroom, noticed Anne seemingly captivated by a strange man in the store. Moving to stand next to Elizabeth, Susan immediately pointed out the handsome stranger to her friend. After studying him, Elizabeth remarked that she thought he looked somewhat like the young man who Anne had dated years ago.

The little window of time spent in Rick's company appeared almost surreal, and Anne began to believe a wall was being torn down between them. Unfortunately, Will returned to inform Elizabeth that Missy Dee was ready to leave, and as he did so, Will quickly took in the scene of Anne and Rick. Stiffening, Anne watched with dread as Will walked territorially towards her.

"Your sister and Susan are leaving now," Will abruptly stated, glaring at Rick as he made this announcement. Will then turned to assist Elizabeth and Susan as they walked towards the door without either of the women saying good-bye to Anne.

Rick stared at Anne, half expecting her to hurry after them. But when she didn't move, Rick asked with surprise, "You're not going with them?"

"There's no room," Anne replied, bringing a puzzled look to Rick's face.

"No room? I'm afraid I'm a bit confused," he confessed.

"Oh!" Anne blushed, "I'm sorry, let me explain. You see our car broke down and Elizabeth and Susan were able to get a lift from our cousin. There isn't enough room for all of us though."

"Surely they don't plan on leaving you here?" Rick asked in an incredulous and protective tone. Anne nodded affirmatively and was going to explain further when Rick spoke with tenderness, "...Anne, as I'm driving my own car," he began, causing a well of hope to spring from her heart. She held her breath as he continued, "I could—"

Will chose that moment to return, interrupting Rick by stating, "Anne, the taxi's here," at which point he sent Rick a challenging look that effectively shattered the magical atmosphere.

This intrusion caused both Anne and Rick to shoot Will unwelcome glances. *Why is Will acting this way?* Anne thought with frustration. Hesitantly, she studied Rick's face, aware that Will's proprietary attitude towards her, coupled by his aimed jealousy towards Rick, might be lending a wrong impression. Trying to gauge what Rick was thinking, Anne's concern appeared to be valid. No longer did Rick's eyes hold the former sweet sparkle or softness shown minutes before. Sadly, the only thing Anne could see now were stiffness and suppressed anger. However, thinking that Rick might possibly be jealous and could care enough to be upset brought a return of happiness to Anne's stricken eyes.

Unfortunately, Rick chose that moment to study Anne's reception of Will and misinterpreted her joy to be attributed to the man's arrival. Wishing to remove himself from this situation as quickly as he could, Rick turned abruptly on his heels and headed towards the checkout counter to complete his purchase.

Anne's elevated mood quickly evaporated. She stood motionless as she watched Rick walk away once again, feeling completely powerless.

"We need to go now," Will urged, flustering Anne with his ill timing.

Ignoring Will's offered hand, Anne knew in her heart that she couldn't leave her former love without saying something. Upon catching Rick steal one last glance in her direction, Anne knew this was her chance. Walking quickly to the checkout, she put her hand on Rick's arm.

"Rick," she appealed, "There's a Fourth of July celebration down at Folsom Lake tomorrow. There'll be fireworks and a live band. My family and I will be going. Maybe you and Harve might like to come?"

Rick's hesitant look made Anne doubtful that he would attend, but before she could say anything more to convince him, Will placed his hand on the small of Anne's back to personally escort her towards the door. Anne was horrified by this possessive gesture but was too emotionally exhausted to fight back. Speechless, Anne felt like a prisoner as Will directed her outside to the taxi, opening the car door for her to enter.

Looking back at the mini-mart, Anne caught sight of Rick watching her through the window. Sighing, Anne climbed inside the vehicle. *What must Rick be thinking?* she thought. As the taxi began pulling away, Anne dared to take one last peek at Rick who was still standing at the window. She prayed she'd be given another opportunity to see him again.

Chapter 39

Anne couldn't sleep that night, tossing back and forth wondering if Rick would show the next day or not. If he didn't come, then when would she ever get another chance to reveal her heart? Of course, she could always send a letter, but how would she then be able to gage Rick's reaction? No, she'd need to talk with him in person to decide whether it was safe enough to share her feelings.

When at last she finally dozed off, Anne's dreams were clouded with images of trying to run to Rick but never being able to move her feet; or trying to locate him in the abyss of her mind and coming up empty-handed. Needless to say, the next morning Anne felt groggy from lack of rest and her attitude wasn't the greatest. Anne was a bit testy having already convinced herself that any chance to reconcile had been lost. Realistically, the chances of Rick attending were quite slim. Despite this pessimistic thinking, Anne still spent extra time in front of the mirror making sure her appearance was flawless, incorporating all the new styling and makeup tricks she had learned thanks to her recent salon visit. Even if Rick wasn't going to be there, she still intended to look her best. Deep down though, she secretly held onto a glimmer of optimism that he might possibly show up for the Fourth of July celebration.

Wanting to disguise the dark circles that had formed the night before, Anne repeatedly checked her appearance using a compact mirror while traveling to Folsom Lake. The lighting in her dad's car was terrible, causing Anne to doubt whether she even wanted to attend. Anne couldn't seem to apply enough coverage to mask her sleep deprived eyes.

"What's up with you?" Elizabeth asked, eyeing Anne suspiciously when they were halfway to the lake. "Who are you trying to impress?"

"What do you mean?" Anne replied defensively as she put down her compact mirror to look at her sister.

"The makeup...the hair...your new look," Elizabeth motioned.

Anne felt like she was on trial. *Is it a crime to want to look nice!?! What is it to Elizabeth anyway? I shouldn't have to explain to her, of all people, why a woman would wish to look her best!* Before Anne could express these unspoken thoughts to her sister, Mr. Elliot spoke up.

"I, for one, am glad Anne has become more concerned about her appearance. After all, we *are* Elliots." Glancing at Anne through the rear-view mirror he added, "For a while there, dear, you were looking a little ragged so this is a refreshing change."

Anne looked away, feeling anxiety fill her inner being. She was beyond exasperated. *First, my family complains when my appearance isn't up to their perceived 'Elliot' standards, and now, when I actually make an effort, they question every little thing! Aaarggh!*

"I didn't realize I'd cause such an uproar by simply opening my compact mirror or wearing a little makeup," began Anne, taking pains to keep her voice calm. "It's simply that I didn't get much sleep last night and I wanted to hide the effects."

Elizabeth shifted away from Anne to pull on her dark sunglasses, signifying the discussion was over while Mr. Elliot turned his attention back to the road where it belonged.

Sighing, Anne began to question whether the possibility of seeing Rick was even worth this scrutiny from her family.

This year's Fourth of July event at Folsom Lake had attracted a large crowd. As Anne got out of vehicle, she surveyed the huge gathering. All of the grassy areas surrounding the lake were now literally cluttered with guests who'd arrived hours in advance just to reserve choice spots on the lawn. Fortunately, her family had the foresight to send Will on ahead to secure a place for them to sit. But now, with all the hundreds of spectators moving about, they were having difficulty locating him. While the others looked in earnest for Will, Anne kept a hopeful eye out for Rick.

"Elizabeth, are you sure that Will planned on getting here early?" Mr. Elliot asked, frustrated while shading his eyes from the bright sun.

With a decided edge to her voice, Elizabeth replied, "Yes, Dad, I'm sure. I just hope Will got a spot close enough to the lake. I hate looking over people…"

"Well, I don't see him anywhere," followed the petulant whine from her father.

Annoyed, Elizabeth stepped forward to scan the crowd with even more determination. Finally, success was met, and with a triumphant look towards her father she boasted, "There he is! I knew we could count on Will, Dad." With a beaming smile, Elizabeth waved to Will as the group edged towards him.

Anne trudged after her family as they maneuvered through the abundant crowd, ever vigil to keep an eye out for Rick or Harve. Moving forward while simultaneously carrying a menagerie of items necessary for her family's comfort, her eyes and heart did a double take. Was that Rick?!? Before she could get another look, several large men managed to block her view. Trying to keep up with her family but determined to confirm her assumption, Anne began walking on her tip-toes in an attempt to see above the flow of traffic. It was situations like this that made her wish she was six feet tall. Finally, a group of children passed by her, allowing Anne only a fraction of time to see what made her insides jump for joy. Not more than thirty feet away was Rick, who, sensing her gaze, looked over. An instant spark of electricity shocked both of them as their eyes locked. It was just the magical moment Anne had been dreaming of.

Standing beside Rick was Harve, who smiled as Anne and Rick unconsciously moved towards each other until they were stationed face to face.

"Rick…" Anne finally said breathlessly, "I'm so glad you decided to come!" They stood there awkwardly while each struggled to think of something to say. Recalling his injury from the fateful day at the beach she asked, "How is your shoulder? Is it fully recovered?"

Rick looked as if her question jolted him back to reality. "Oh…" he mumbled as he moved it in full rotation. "Better. I have my full range back."

Anne nodded and bit her lip nervously.

"Oh, that reminds me," Rick added. "Did you hear the good news about Louise and Ben? Who would have guessed an engagement would have resulted from her accident?"

Hearing Rick refer to Ben and Louise's plans of marriage as "good news" cheered Anne's heart. It made her think perhaps Admiral Croft had been correct in supposing Rick never cared for Louise in that way.

"Yes!" Anne smiled. "The Admiral told me. I was really surprised. I hope they'll be very happy."

"Me, too," Rick smiled in return. "They are fortunate that both families approve." As Rick said these words, he glanced pointedly towards her father. Anne felt she understood his meaning as he continued, "It just makes things easier when there is no opposition. Even so, I am surprised at how quickly their love has come about. Don't get me wrong, Louise is a great girl, but after all, Ben was still recovering from a broken heart…you see, his fiancé, Francie, was such an incredible woman...a man does not simply forget someone like that. If he does, then I'd have to question the depth of his love."

The gentleness behind Rick's eyes as he voiced these words mesmerized Anne, making her incapable of looking away. *Could there be a deeper meaning behind his words?* she thought as she stood before Rick bright-eyed, feeling as though she were eighteen years old again.

"Anne," Rick tenderly spoke her name, "I have never..." he paused.

Anne waited breathlessly to hear more and the stillness seemed like an eternity...

KA-BOOM! A spectacular opening firework blasted into the sky, exploding as it sent shimmers of light everywhere. The beautiful display normally would have caused Anne much delight, but the timing could not have been worse as it interrupted Rick mid-sentence. Between the noise of the fireworks and the ensuing appreciation from the crowd, it made the hearing of Rick's words next to impossible.

"Ladies and gentleman," began the host from his platform on the stage, "Welcome to this year's Fourth of July celebration!"

"Anne!"

But this time it was not Rick's strong and tender voice calling her name, but rather the shrill voice of Elizabeth. With dread, Anne looked over to her sister who was standing nearby with her hands on her hips looking displeased. Apparently Anne's interaction with Rick was causing a spectacle, and her sister was not the only one who had noticed. Her father and the others were observing them as well, but more out of curiosity.

"The show's starting!" Elizabeth's voice was laced with veiled contempt towards Rick as she issued what seemed like a command for Anne to join them.

Anne turned back to Rick who now spoke with disparity. "As *always*, your family wants you," he said, his body language indicating whatever moment had just been happening between them no longer existed. *Oh, will the two of us ever get that second chance I feel we both desire?* thought Anne as her eyes shimmered with tears she refused to shed. Now was not the time to get emotional.

Glancing back at her family, Anne's heart tightened when she saw Rick already moving back to rejoin Harve. Anne felt as if her world were falling apart, but even so, she continued to hold out a glimmer of hope that Rick still cared, else why did he come tonight?

As she settled onto the blanket Will had laid out for their family, Anne belatedly wished that she had invited Rick and Harve to join their party. Even if they hadn't been able to talk, Anne felt she could have communicated volumes by her behavior towards Rick.

"What do you keep looking at?" Will asked Anne with a hint of annoyance at being ignored. Anne had been too wrapped up in keeping an eye on Rick to worry about what the others were thinking around her.

"Oh...um," Anne began, trying to force her eyes away from Rick so that she could answer Will but was reluctant to do so.

Seeing that her attention was still divided, Will placed his finger on the top of Anne's hand to trace it seductively up her arm. The sensation sent chills down her spine—the type of chills you get though when watching a horror flick. Startled at this intimate gesture, Anne quickly pulled her hand away, hoping Rick by chance hadn't witnessed Will's forward touch.

"I'm just taking everything in, crowds included," Anne explained while sending Will a questioning look.

But Will was not so easily duped. Since Anne's arrival, he had noticed her preoccupied behavior. He also was aware Anne kept looking in the direction of the man previously seen at the mini-mart.

Trying a different approach to secure the answers he wanted, Will turned to Mr. Elliot. "Who's that guy over there?" he asked, motioning to Rick in the distance. "The one Anne was talking to earlier."

Walter looked as directed, straining his eyes to see the person Will was referring to, but it was Elizabeth who answered the question, "Oh, *him*...that's Rick Wentworth."

At the mention of Rick's name, Mr. Elliot became alert, squinting even harder as Elizabeth unenthusiastically pointed Wentworth out to her dad. "Really?" he said with surprise at catching sight of him, "I would never have recognized him."

"If you'd wear your glasses like you're supposed to, you wouldn't have that problem," Elizabeth retorted, settling back into her lawn chair.

"But they make me look old," Mr. Elliot pouted.

Having obtained the information he sought, Will pointedly moved back to sit close to Anne, making sure Rick noticed the gesture while sending a malicious look of triumph his way.

By that time, the band had begun playing the tune "What Are You Doing the Rest of Your Life?" Will listened to the first stanza. Since the words to the song served his purpose nicely, he decided to make the most of this opportune moment. Securing her attention, he pointedly asked, "Anne...what are you doing for the rest of your life?"

Obtuse to his meaning, Anne absentmindedly responded, "Oh yes, I like that song, too."

A shockwave of anger rippled down Will's spine as he watched Anne once again turn her attention back to her present favorite activity: keeping an eye on that fellow named Rick. "No!" he exclaimed more sharply then he had intended, causing Anne to look his way. Noting the frightened look in her eyes, he quickly softened his tone to one of tenderness. "Dearest Anne, I was asking you a question. What are *you* doing...for the rest of your life?"

Anne looked at him rather confused. "Huh?" she asked, not getting his meaning.

Will was having trouble keeping his irritation under wraps due to Anne making this more difficult than expected. He quickly channeled his MTV experience to mask his displeasure, picking up her hand and stroking it with tenderness. "Anne," Will began, "What would you say if I told you I wanted to love and pamper you for the rest of *your* life?"

Anne tried to pull her hand away, but Will's tight grip refused to lessen. Thinking Rick might be observing this tête-à-tête, she worried he might misunderstand. To make matters worse, Will placed his other hand directly on Anne's cheek, forcing her to look into his eyes.

"Will...what is this all about?" Anne asked, now completely bewildered—not only by his words, but also by his actions.

"Anne, I envision the two of us—" Will started to say, but Anne didn't hear the rest.

Out of the corner of her eye, Anne witnessed Rick turning to leave with Harve, causing panic to set in. Struggling against the hold Will had on her, Anne managed to get free.

"Anne!" Will yelled with a combination of frustration and astonishment at seeing Anne scramble after the departing Rick.

As Will was heralding Anne, she was shouting out to Rick, hoping the latter would slow down enough for her to catch him in the crowded park.

Luckily, Rick heard his name and turned in time to see Anne rushing towards him. Stopping his progress, Rick spoke briefly to Harve who nodded. His friend then proceeded on to give the two some space.

"Leaving so soon?" Anne asked breathlessly and with some trepidation when she reached him.

"Yes," Rick bit out the word, his voice an emotionless pit.

Anne's mind went blank. What could she say to convince him not to leave? She somehow sensed Rick would be unreceptive to any of her entreaties. It was only when Anne felt a touch on her shoulder that she realized Will had followed her, filling Anne with a sense of doom. By Will's pursuit of her, he effectively signed, sealed, and delivered Rick's good-bye.

"Anne...*dear*, please come back," Will pleaded, his voice causing Anne's blood to boil at the addition of the word "dear".

Rick didn't wait to hear Anne's reply and began to walk away. Not wasting a moment, she moved swiftly in front of Rick's exit route, not caring how her actions appeared.

"...but the fireworks, they're not even half way through!" Anne gasped. Then taking one more leap of faith she pleaded, "Please, can't you stay?"

"There's no reason anymore," Rick replied, his eyes portraying the closed state of his heart.

It felt as if the wind had been knocked out of her. Anne stood there feeling the hurt of his words—*so I'm not enough of a reason for him to stay...* the thought slowly penetrated Anne's mind. *Here I've pined for Rick for nearly eight years and this is how I am to remember him and be remembered?*

"Anne," Will interrupted the depressing thoughts. "Speaking of fireworks, we're standing in the way. We need to go sit down."

Anne, who was normally courteous, couldn't have cared less at this point about blocking other people's views. She was also extremely irritated at Will since he was most likely the cause for the cool demeanor Rick was now exhibiting.

"Don't worry," Rick said, looking between the two of them pointedly and adding harshly, "I've *seen* enough. Now excuse me so that I can be on my way."

Anne's shoulders slumped as she watched Rick aggressively move past her without even a backwards glance, disappearing into the crowd and out of her life. She stood there deflated and drained as if the very essence of her had been removed. Anne remained in this state until Will jarred her back to reality when he circled his arm around her shoulders, expressing a wish to head back. Will's touch seared her. Anne was shocked to find how repugnant Will now was to her when merely days ago he seemed handsome and entertaining. Everything in her wanted to push Will away but was too weary to fight.

Her dad chose that moment to appear, carrying three ice cream cones in tow. "Good! I've found you!" Mr. Elliot said as he approached, totally oblivious to what had happened merely seconds before. "Ice cream anyone?"

Although indulging in ice cream seemed like a great antidote for a broken heart, it held no remedy for Anne. However, the rare kindness shown by her father proved too much for Anne and without warning, despite her resolve to stay strong, she burst into tears and fled.

Walter stood there perplexed. "Did I choose the wrong flavor? That's not like Anne to be so picky," he bemoaned with an injured tone. Mr. Elliot turned to Will for sympathy but found none. Will also declined the offered cone as the young man followed in haste after the distraught Anne. Her dad frowned, "Now what am I going to do with the two extra cones? Has everyone around here gone bonkers? Good gravy! This is Haagen-Dazs we're talking about!"

Chapter 40

Fortunately for Anne, she had visitors to occupy her time and mind. Mary, Charles, and the boys had arrived, as well as Etta and Mrs. Musgrove.

Since Anne was to be one of Etta's bridesmaids, she was quickly recruited to help with arrangements for Etta's forthcoming wedding. Anne felt grateful for this occupation as it filled her days with enough activity to avoid almost all interactions with Will and Rick. Etta was all aflutter at having such an abundance of bridal selections at her fingertips while staying in California. Etta and her mother heavily relied on Anne's attendance at the numerous appointments with cake makers, decoration warehouses, florists, and most importantly, wedding dress boutiques.

On this particular day, they were at their fourth dress shop with Etta gazing at herself in a full length mirror. Anne tried not to be bored, but just at this location alone Etta had tried on at least two dozen or more selections. As Etta returned to the dressing room, Anne sat in a corner, resting her eyes from all the excitement while Mary preferred to look through magazines. Not wanting to feel left out, Mary had tagged along even though her complaints had become a constant occurrence. Luckily, this bridal boutique had a gossip magazine full of pictures to keep Mary occupied for the time being.

"Anne!" Etta called out, jarring Anne from her rest.

"Hmm?" Anne responded rather absentmindedly, not bothering to look up. If Anne was to be honest, she considered Etta a bit excessive in her search for the ultimate dress. During the past two hours alone, Etta had declared five different dresses to be 'the one', only to later change her mind. Although this was aggravating, Anne tried to remind herself that perhaps she might be as tiresome when her time came. At this reflection, Anne suddenly stopped short. An unwelcome thought came to her mind...*but will I ever get to be a bride? What if marriage never happens for me?* These thoughts depressed Anne greatly, since at this point, matrimony seemed highly unlikely.

"Well, what do you think?" an animated Etta squeaked with newfound excitement. There upon a pedestal, Etta stood, reverently stroking the soft, white sheathy material of the dress. It shimmered with beauty and gathered becomingly at Etta's waist as the folds of the gown worked magic to enhance her already lovely form. To complete this stunning dress, an exquisite and very lengthy train flowed behind, showcasing impeccable bead work.

The sight took Anne's breath away. Etta looked fantastic in the gown—a picture of perfection. "Oh, Etta...it's magnificent!" Anne exclaimed.

Mary, at hearing the awe in Anne's voice, took a moment to tear her eyes away from the scandal magazine to bestow her approval. "Wow, Etta, you look incredible!"

Judging by Etta's smile, Anne presumed the search for the ultimate dress was complete. To cement Anne's intuition, Mrs. Musgrove and her daughter embraced one other, tears brimming in Clara's eyes.

While the two finalized a few needed alterations with the seamstress, Anne looked wistfully through the dresses, wondering if one day, she too, would have the opportunity to wear a wedding gown. Although the selections before her were beautiful and elegant, it had always been Anne's dream to wear her mother's dress. Anne had discovered the vintage gown while packing up the house in Oregon. Not being able to resist trying it on, Anne was ecstatic to find it fit perfect, almost as if it had been made especially for her. But with her 26th birthday fast approaching, Anne felt as if her young, girlish dreams were quickly evaporating. The final blow had been Rick's rejection at the Fourth of July celebration. Anne had always held out hope that despite their long separation it would be Rick she'd one day walk down the aisle to—and now that dream had been destroyed.

Anne's stomach growled, reminding her it had been hours since her last meal. Looking at her watch, she realized it was almost time for the girls to meet up with Charles, Rick and Harve for lunch. The idea of being around Rick almost made Anne's appetite vanish, but she would suck it up, at least for her stomach's sake.

"Ready?" Mary asked Anne when she finally located her sister wedged between two tight aisles of wedding gowns, "I'm starving!"

Anne nodded and followed Mary out of the maze, hoping the meal would be worth the pain of being in Rick's company.

"Where are the kids?" Charles asked Mary when they all finally met up at the mall's restaurant.

"With my dad. He took them to a movie," Mary replied from behind her menu. She couldn't decide between the Biggie's Buffalo Burger or the Spicy Sausage Spaghetti.

Charles nodded and then accepted Anne's offer to vacate the seat next to Mary so he could be near his wife. Rick and Harve had already seated themselves, so Anne cringed when she realized the only spot left was next to Rick. *Just my luck*, Anne thought as she slowly sat down.

Rick inclined his head in her direction, but to Anne's relief she was spared an acknowledgment by the arrival of the waitress who greeted everyone with a kind smile. "It looks like your party is all here now? Are you ready to order or should I give you a few minutes to look over the menu?" she inquired politely. The group indicated they needed more time, and the server left to check on her other tables.

"Did you find a dress, Etta?" Charles asked his little sister after deciding on his selection for lunch.

The glow on Etta's face was answer enough, but she left no doubt when she excitedly began to describe the dress in vivid detail. Anne smiled and listened, but periodically allowed her eyes to sneak peeks at Rick. To Anne's surprise, during one of her glances, he leaned towards her and began to speak in a hushed tone. Breathless, Anne listened.

"So...when am I to wish you congratulations?" he asked, avoiding eye contact.

"Congratulations...for what?" she whispered back in confusion. Anne found herself not only flustered by Rick's close proximity, but was now perplexed by his question as well.

"Your engagement to Will Elliot," he stated matter-of-factly, his voice flat and infused with a hint of accusation.

"What are you talking about?" Anne asked flabbergasted, trying to piece together the puzzle his words had created. This didn't make sense. She wasn't engaged to Will! And who would spread such a rumor?

"Charles told me the two of you will most likely wed this fall," Rick answered, flipping over his menu as if totally uninterested in her reply.

Dumbfounded, Anne croaked, "What! Why on earth would Charles say such a thing?" Rick's head jerked up at Anne's vehement response, causing him to look at her with surprise. Anne met his eyes squarely, and continued, "I'm no—"

"Are you ready?" interrupted a voice. Both turned to see the waitress all set to take orders. Trying to be calm, yet feeling anything but, Anne looked at her menu to quickly scan for an item to select.

"I'll start with you," the server said, motioning to Rick.

Looking a bit shaken, Rick nodded and reached for the menu. After a quick perusal, he said, "I'll have the...um... the Santa Fe Burrito."

The waitress wrote it down then turned to take Anne's order.

"Anne!" Mary exclaimed dramatically. Anne at first wondered if Mary was upset she was taking too long to order, but how could that be when the waitress had just given Anne her full attention? The wild-eyed gaze on Mary's face however told Anne the outburst was due to something entirely different.

"I think I see Will Elliot!" Mary said, motioning to the window. "Come, look!"

Anne realized Mary wanted her to confirm the observation, but with Rick watching, it would be extremely awkward, if not downright embarrassing. Anne attempted to dissuade her sister, "I don't see how it could be. He told me he was to be out of town for the next few days on business."

With the waitress still standing patiently in front of her, Anne turned her attention back to the menu. But Mary wasn't giving up that easily.

"I'm certain it's him. Please come and look!" Mary persisted.

Anne sighed, knowing her sister would not quit until she got her way. "I'll have the Thai Salad," she told the waitress and then reluctantly moved to join Mary at the window.

Once there, Anne looked down at the busy street below. The amount of traffic was mind boggling. The four driving lanes looked more like a highway with rushing commuters hurrying to get back to work before their lunch time was up. Along the street were several upscale shops where many pedestrians could be seen. Mary instructed Anne to gaze near the entrance of Ralph Lauren. Sure enough, standing before a display window was the one and only Will Elliot.

Mary's look was not only smug, but also triumphant at seeing her sister's astonishment. "And isn't that Susan Clay standing next to him?" she asked with curiosity. "I thought he didn't like her."

Taking a closer look, there was no mistaking the woman next to Will—it was indeed Susan. In fact, the two looked rather on good terms as Susan openly flirted while pointing to an item through a shop's window that she apparently liked.

"Yes, you're right..." Anne said in puzzlement, and Mary nodded in agreement. *Why would Will need to lie about being out of town?* she thought. *And even more of a mystery...why is he with Susan?*

Despite meaning to, Anne found her curiosity aroused and momentarily forgot about the interrupted conversation with Rick. But that was not the case for him. With Anne distracted, Rick was able to study her unguarded, taking considerable interest in Anne's behavior. He took pains to observe both her demeanor and also her response at discovering that the *rat* was in town, and worse—with another woman. Judging by Anne's reaction, Rick felt there must be some truth in what Charles had told him, otherwise why would Anne invest such notice in what was happening below. What he couldn't understand was why she would give her heart to someone so untrustworthy? It gave Rick just one more reason to hate the man.

Chapter 41

Once the group had finished lunch, they strolled down the same street where Will and Susan had been seen earlier. Although the two in question were long since gone, Anne still couldn't shake the odd feeling at seeing them together. One thing Anne knew for certain was that Will must be up to something so she made a mental note to be on guard.

"Anne," Charles called to her, gaining her attention. "We were all thinking about seeing a play next Friday. Would you like to join us?"

Anne brightened at the suggestion. She hadn't gone to a theatre in ages, and the idea sounded great. Just as she was about to accept, Anne's excitement quickly evaporated when she recalled a prior obligation. A charity to raise funds for the American Cancer Society was being held in their home, an event her father planned annually since his wife's death. Because it involved gambling, Anne wasn't too enthusiastic about it, but to honor both her dad and departed mother, she had agreed to assist where needed.

"Well, if it were up to me, I'd love to go," Anne began, "But Dad asked me to help out with the benefit he's hosting for charity. In fact, didn't Elizabeth mention anything to you? Dad specifically asked her to do so."

"Oh, a game night does sound like fun, Charles," Mary said, turning to her husband in anticipation. "Let's go see the play some other night."

"I don't see why not. And as long as they have poker, I'm good," Charles answered, looking to Anne for confirmation to which she nodded in agreement.

"Cool! This means we can all see Anne's new home!" Etta smiled kindly at Anne. "Is it really near a vineyard?"

Anne nodded and when asked for more details, she described the many acres of planted grapes wrapped around their home. Mary became impatient at all the attention focused on her sister. With deliberation, Mary interrupted to point out a dress boutique, knowing it would awaken the voracious shopping habit of Etta. Mary was not disappointed. Etta immediately excused herself to check out the store with Mary accompanying her. As the two ladies went to get a better look, Rick took the opportunity to move closer to Anne.

"So your dad is still hosting those game parties?" Rick asked.

"Um, yes," Anne said, a little flustered at his approach. "Yet I've never appreciated the way he raises money. Too much like Las Vegas for me," she confessed.

Rick smiled knowingly, which made Anne's heart somersault. "No, you never did care for games of chance, did you?" he said tenderly.

Anne was touched that Rick would remember such an insignificant thing about her, especially after all this time. Hearing him speak as he had, the pain Anne had been harboring from their last two encounters began to slowly peel away. A budding hope started to once again manifest itself in her heart. *After all, doesn't that show he once cared?* she thought longingly. *How pitiful I am!* Anne chided herself. *The slightest bit of attention from Rick and the next thing I'm convincing myself there's still a chance for the two of us!* Looking expectedly at Rick, Anne waited for him to continue.

"Let's get a move on, ladies," Charles said to the group as he clapped his hands together. "You've done enough shopping for today...any more and I'll be broke," he chuckled.

Herding the group towards the parking lot, Mary sent her husband a scathing look letting him know she wasn't at all pleased. Anne sighed. For what seemed like the umpteenth time, the moment had been lost for any sort of reconciliation. Anne needed answers for all those silent years, or even closure for that matter, if indeed that's what Rick desired. Anne was almost beginning to feel as though destiny was having a hand in keeping them apart. At every opportunity in which Rick would start to address their past, he was interrupted; and every time she thought she saw the walls begin to tumble down, they went right back up again. It was frustrating for Anne to say the least, and it didn't particularly make her a fan of destiny at that moment.

Chapter 42

With only a few days left before Carol made her return to Portland, she and Anne began to spend as much quality time together as possible. Anne had been delighted when Carol made the decision to remain longer than her initial plan, extending her visit to almost a month.

On this beautiful morning, the two had decided to share tea in the family room, as its large bay windows afforded a breathtaking view of a nearby vineyard. What started out as an enjoyable time of tea and conversation reminiscing about Anne's mother and their mutual joy of cooking, had now turned into a subject Anne wished to avoid—the topic of Will. Anne inwardly kicked herself when she inadvertently mentioned Will's name while discussing a family event. As Anne suspected, this was just the opening Carol was waiting for.

Carol was bent on Anne securing a husband, especially one she could approve of. To Carol, Will appeared to be the best candidate. So far he seemed to be a perfect gentleman and a man well capable of taking care of Anne the way she deserved to be treated. Yet, Anne couldn't shake her uneasy feeling about Will. Not only that, she was still somewhat annoyed at how territorial he became around Rick. As antici-pated, Carol seized this opportunity to request an update on all of Anne's latest interactions with Will. Although Anne could speak of some fun times she had shared with Will, what she really wanted to do was discuss a number of red flags she had observed. However, Anne knew it would be pointless as Carol would devise ways to overlook them. Sadly, Carol was blinded by an six letter word, S-T-A-T-U-S.

"Maybe all this is in your favor," began Carol after hearing the surprising news Anne had picked up from Jane, plus the comment Rick had made about an impending engagement. "Will must have said something to either your dad or Charles. Why else would Rick think you two were getting married? Anne, this is so exciting!" Carol said, taking Anne's hand. "You're getting engaged! Just think of the possibilities, perhaps even a wedding at a local vineyard." Carol's eyes were bright with excitement, and it was making Anne extremely nervous. "He'll probably take you to Hawaii on your honeymoon," continued Carol, "Maybe you can persuade him to live in Portland so you can be near me."

This was moving way too fast for Anne. She didn't even know if she wanted to consider Will as husband material— nor was she even sure if he was trustworthy!

"Whoa! First of all, you're forgetting I never said yes to his 'indirect' proposal." As soon as the words left Anne's mouth, she knew she had used the wrong word choice at seeing Carol's sassy smile and "ahh ha" expression. Backtracking, Anne continued, "What I meant to say is that he *started* to propose but then got interrupted."

Anne had only made it worse. Carol kept smiling her Cheshire-cat look, not saying a word, which exasperated Anne all the more.

"Alright...then how do you explain that I saw him with Susan at the mall when he told my family he'd be out of town?" Anne challenged, hoping it would help Carol better understand why she was so wary of Will.

There was also another reason why Anne found herself resisting Will, but even Anne didn't want to voice it. Despite all that had gone down the past few months with Rick, even after being wounded greatly by his behavior, she still found herself very much in love with him.

"I'm sure there's a perfectly good reason," Carol responded to Anne's earlier question.

"Like what?" Anne questioned. Carol always had an explanation.

"Well...perhaps he...he didn't want you to know he was in town so he could surprise you with an engagement ring. Maybe Susan was helping him pick one out."

Anne rested her head back onto the sofa cushion behind her. She had to admit Carol had actually come up with a plausible excuse, but somehow Anne couldn't quite buy into it. Hesitantly, Anne responded, "You could be right, but I can't shake the feeling he was up to something other than getting me a ring."

"What have you got against Will, Anne?" Carol asked. "He's perfect for you."

Anne lifted her head to look at Carol again. "I'll grant you that he's handsome and charming. In fact, he's really too perfect. Maybe that's why I just don't trust him."

Carol raised her eyebrows quizzically and drank a sip of her still warm chamomile tea. Anne relaxed, knowing Carol wouldn't push the subject further, at least for the time being.

Taking a sip of her own tea, Anne let her eyes wander to the beautiful scene outdoors. As she watched the gentle breeze move the flowers to a slow, rhythmic sway, Anne reflected that if Rick hadn't come back into her life, perhaps she might have been persuaded to consider Will more seriously. After all, he was extremely good-looking, possessed an interesting personality, and had wealth to boot. Will was an excellent catch. *Am I being too romantic in wanting to hold out for a dream? I mean, there's no certainty Rick will ever again return my feelings,* Anne thought. *Maybe I'm being foolish to ignore such an eligible man as Will...*

Looking again at her godmother, Anne tried to convince herself that maybe Carol was right.

Chapter 43

After Anne's conversation with Carol it was becoming almost impossible to avoid Will. It was as if he had somehow sensed Anne's concerns, and doubled his efforts to woo her. Will was constantly around the house, attaching himself to Anne and making his intentions all too clear. What made things worse was Will had the full support of both Mr. Elliot and Carol, and therefore just needed Anne to jump on board—something she had no intention of doing. The thought of marriage to Will somehow terrified her, making Anne diligent to never allow him to be alone with her, even if that meant spending time in Elizabeth's company. Anne wasn't going to place herself in a situation where he'd have a chance to *formally* pop the question.

Anne wished she could turn to Carol for sympathy or support, but her dear friend only saw Will's outer appearance and wealth. Carol made no secret she was already devising wedding preparations. Anne nearly had a panic attack after discovering that her godmother had covertly taken pictures of the two of them, later uploading them into a program showing what their future children would look like! When apprehended, the guilty Carol promised never to do it again, especially since it was causing Anne to become even more resistant to Will. And Anne's hesitation was not due to their "supposed" children looking bad, quite the contrary, but it made her feel pressured, and that was something Anne did not like.

It was times like these that Anne found solace in the company of her dear friend Jane, where the drama could be left behind and more important things could be focused on.

Sadly, Anne had experienced another rough day with Carol. It started with her godmother probing, "You know, Etta chose red and brown for her wedding colors. What would you have chosen?" Although Carol presumed she had underhandedly gotten away with asking another wedding question, it was not the case.

Anne decided to turn the question around, "Why do you ask?" she inquired, even though she knew the reason why. Just the other night Anne had overheard her godmother on the phone with a wedding planner. The discussion had stalled when the planner asked what colors would be used for the ceremony. Carol needed this vital information to continue her dastardly plans.

"Oh...just curious," Carol didn't seem to miss a beat.

"Carol! I know exactly what you're up to!" Anne accused, "I am *not* getting married to Will!"

Despite Anne's continued efforts to curtail her godmother from trying to push her into marriage, Carol was having a difficult time understanding why Anne simply couldn't enjoy the idea of a beau. However, Anne wasn't the type of girl to toy with a man's feelings. In order for her to reciprocate Will's regard (and that was assuming his devotion was genuine), she'd have to believe herself committed and in love with him. Right now, her mind and heart belonged to another, so in no way could Anne, with any honesty, contemplate such a serious step as matrimony with Will.

So, it was with a heavy heart that Anne showed up at her friend's room for a visit. Jane immediately sensed something was wrong, and with a little prodding, Anne began to open up to her.

"I don't know why everybody thinks I'm going to marry Will! I don't even really know him that well!" Anne complained, getting all worked up, but appreciating how she could finally share her true feelings with someone.

"But hasn't he already popped the question?" Jane asked searchingly.

"Well, yes and no," Anne said with a grimace, "Will has not officially asked me, but even if he did, I don't know what I would say...at least not at this point. Honestly, I don't know if it's just bad timing or whether I'd ever want to marry him. I feel trapped, plus I still have all these doubts about Will that make it almost impossible for me to consider him seriously..."

Anne pondered why Jane wasn't trying to convince her she needed to be with Will like everyone else. It felt refreshing to say the least. However, if Will was as good as most people thought, why couldn't Anne see it? *And why does the idea of "forever" with him make me so uncomfortable?* she wondered. *Am I being unreasonable?*

But before Anne could voice these questions, Nurse Rooke entered the room with a glass of water and Jane's afternoon snack.

"So, if he does ask, which I am sure he will, you don't think you'd say yes?" Jane inquired, not letting the Nurse's entrance distract her.

"I...couldn't...I don't love him," Anne responded.

Having committed this statement out loud somehow broke the chains that had been like weights holding her captive. The sensation was freeing to Anne and she felt as if a great burden had been lifted. True, Anne had liked the attention and admiration she received from Will as a suitor, but he hadn't been able to touch her heart—and no persuasion could make her throw her life away just for the comfortable existence he could offer.

As Jane watched the transformation take place on Anne's face, she clasped her hands together joyfully. "Nurse Rooke, she's not engaged to him!" Jane announced with excitement.

"Thank heavens!" Nurse Rooke heartily resounded, sharing an equally satisfied look with her patient.

While Jane took a sip of water to moisten her dry throat after the highly charged announcement, Anne observed the two women carefully. It seemed odd that they appeared not only joyous, but relieved at Anne's spoken refusal towards any future advances from Will.

"Um, wow...it means a lot that you are both so supportive of my feelings and not trying to change my mind," Anne said, still dazed by their elated attitudes on the "non-engagement" news.

Jane took Anne's hand, and with a glance at her caregiver said, "Nurse Rooke, perhaps it's time you tell Anne what you know."

Nurse Rooke nodded. Moving towards the bed, she sat on the edge nearest Anne and leaned closer for "confidentiality".

"Well," she started dramatically, "I was changing the diaper of Mrs. Wallis' baby in the nursery yesterday, and, if I may say so, it was quite nasty."

Anne scrunched her face in puzzlement. *This was what Jane wanted me to hear? How odd...*

"The baby had way too much soy in her diet," Nurse Rooke explained, expecting acknowledgment from Jane. Instead, Jane returned a look which signaled the nurse was getting off topic, so her caregiver quickly resumed course. "Anyway, I overheard Mr. Wallis tell Mrs. Wallis that Will had asked him for *another* loan."

With that, Nurse Rooke stood up, raising her eyebrows to look knowingly at Jane. Jane nodded her approval of the caregiver's account, then turned to Anne for feedback.

"A loan?" Anne asked. "I don't understand. Will is supposedly well off."

"Not any more!" Jane exclaimed.

"Dear, you need to know that currently the life Will's living is a sham," Nurse Rooke stated matter-of-factly.

"But what about the income he makes from the MTV show?" Anne asked, "Surely that provides more than enough money for him."

"Ratings have been worse than expected. Not only that, Will invested his own funds in the show," Jane explained, "And it doesn't have the needed sponsors to stay afloat."

"But if Will doesn't have any money of his own, then why would he…" Anne's voice trailed off as Jane and her caregiver watched her with anxious eyes. Anne didn't have to finish, she knew the answer to her own question. She felt used. "You mean Will has only been after me for my mother's inheritance?" she spit out the words with contempt.

Jane nodded sadly. "But only in part," she began. "Think about it, Anne. If it was totally for the money, then why not choose your sister who already likes him? There would have been no problem in securing her hand." Anne nodded, knowing she was right. "No, dear, I really do believe he has an attraction to you," Jane reassured.

Anne slowly got up and began to repeatedly pace the width of the room. Stopping abruptly, she turned and faced the ladies. "Why are there so many cads out there? Are there no decent men left?"

Jane and Nurse Rooke looked to Anne in sympathy while Anne sat down in a huff.

"*That's* why I never married," Nurse Rooke commented with a justified and rather pious look before taking a large bite of the cookie left untouched by Jane.

Observing the caregiver's masculine build and faint mustache, Anne guessed there were probably other reasons why she hadn't married—but kept them to herself. Sitting up, Anne raised a high-five in the air, "Amen to that!"

Chapter 44

Drawn to an exquisite floral display, Anne lingered to smell some roses while en route to the hotel where the Musgrove's were staying. She'd decided to drive the back roads into Sacramento, and upon spying a local fresh flower stand couldn't resist pulling over. The farmer had a wide variety of colorful tulips, cute daisies, intoxicating hydrangeas, and more. Anne was in flower heaven. Selecting several bunches of the vibrant tulips, lilies, and roses, she decided to put together a bouquet for Clara, thinking how much the dear lady must miss her gardens from home. Anne enjoyed their sweet fragrance as she finished her commute into town.

Clara opened the hotel door to see Anne holding the lovely arrangement of flowers.

"Anne, come on in!" she exclaimed, "What a gorgeous bouquet!"

"They're for you. I thought you'd enjoy something to remind you of home," Anne smiled as she presented them to Mrs. Musgrove.

"Just what I needed! You are such a sweet dear," Clara smiled, her eyes declaring her home-sickness. "Etta and your sister left to run a few errands, but they should be back soon, and Charles took the boys to an aquarium."

Anne nodded and stepped inside, following Clara to the kitchenette area where Mrs. Musgrove managed to find a vase in which to display the flowers.

"Etta can't wait to show off the bridesmaid's dress she got for you," Clara said with a wink.

Glancing about the hotel suite, Anne became aware that she and Clara weren't alone. Standing by the window was Harve, whose attention was fastened to a piece of paper in his hand. Sitting at the room's desk not far from him was Rick, who was diligently writing. Anne turned to Mrs. Musgrove in puzzlement.

Clara immediately apologized for her lapse in manners. "Oh, Anne, I got so excited by the flowers I forgot to inform you of our guests. What with both of these gentlemen being involved in Louise's wedding, I invited them for lunch hoping to get a fresh update on the wedding plans. Plus, Harve is headed back to Lincoln City tomorrow and he was nice enough to agree to take back some items I purchase for Louise."

Harve looked up at that moment to smile at Anne. "Hi, there," he greeted warmly, forcing Rick to acknowledge Anne with a quick but courteous nod of his head before returning back to his task.

Anne tried not to take his lack of enthusiasm personally, but it was hard not to—especially when she recalled the way Rick used to light up in her presence. The smiles he gave back then were so gentle they made her heart skip a beat every time he flashed them her way. Those special moments would stay with her forever.

On the television, Anne could hear the familiar sounds of *The Price Is Right*. Knowing it was one of Clara's favorite shows, Anne wasn't surprised when Mrs. Musgrove asked if she could finish watching the program. "Anne, would you think me rude if I ignored you for a moment? They're just about ready to do the final showcase, and that's my favorite part."

Anne smiled, "Of course, don't mind me—I'll go bother Harve for a bit."

With Clara's attention riveted by the television, Anne headed towards Harve. As expected, Harve's easygoing attitude instantly made her feel welcome.

"My best man speech," Harve said, pointing to the paper he was holding in his hand. "Or at least it will be when I am finished. Rick over there is writing his as well, actually." In explanation, Harve added, "Ben couldn't make up his mind which to choose, so he made both of us his best man."

"That sounds just like him," Anne chuckled before seeing the almost imperceptible change in Harve's demeanor. She couldn't quite put her finger on it, but it was almost as if he was melancholy. "I hope you don't mind me asking, but is everything okay?" Anne queried.

Acknowledging his altered mood, Harve looked at her kindly, thinking to himself what an intuitive woman Anne was. There were few besides his wife Melissa or Rick who could read him so well. Making sure Clara's attention was securely attached to the television, he lowered his voice to explain, knowing Anne would keep his confidence.

"I must admit this is a very difficult chore for me," Harve began, "Knowing that less than a year ago Ben was engaged to my sister. To think this should have been their wedding…"

Anne immediately understood and felt her heart break at witnessing the deep sadness in Harve's sorrowful eyes. It was obvious Francie's death still affected him, and Anne was genuinely touched by the deep affection Harve held for his late sister.

"I know Francie wouldn't have forgotten *him* so easily," Harve finished quietly, looking down to play with the paper in his hand.

"No woman who truly loves can forget," Anne said with sincerity.

Unobserved by either of them, Rick ceased to write. Instead, his attention was diverted to that of listening in on their conversation once he became aware of their topic. Despite himself, Rick was anxious to know whether Anne was speaking in general, or from experience.

"Not the good ones anyway," Harve continued, "I don't think that applies to all women though."

Anne shook her head in disagreement. "We don't forget men as easily as they forget us." Harve's dubious look encouraged Anne to further defend her stance. "A man can suppress his emotions, whereas a woman's are always on the surface and no amount of distraction can override them."

The sound of Rick's knee hitting the desk prompted Anne and Harve to seek the source of the noise. Noting the flushed look on Rick's cheeks and his somewhat nervous demeanor, Harve assumed Rick was hinting it was time to leave.

"Are you ready to go?" he asked Rick.

"Ahh...no, just a few minutes more," Rick answered in distraction as he hurriedly grabbed a new piece of paper and began to write furiously. Harve thought it strange, but shrugged and resumed his conversation with Anne.

"I find it hard to accept that men are less committed then women," Harve continued, bating Anne. "I believe the reverse. Men cannot forget those they love. Every man I know tells me how fickle the nature of a woman is."

"Yes, but your view is very one-sided," Anne replied pointedly.

"As is yours," he retorted.

Anne began to wonder if Rick had ever confided in Harve regarding their former relationship. Did he blame Anne for her supposed "fickleness" in the breakup? After all, it seemed obvious from their initial meeting that Harve and his wife had heard Anne's name before. Perhaps this was Harve's attempt at satisfying his curiosity? She now wished the debate to end, and hoped to settle the topic by stating, "Then I guess we must agree to disagree."

Harve acquiesced to Anne's suggestion, although he still wanted to add more on this subject. "I hope though, you understand that not all men move on so easily," Harve persisted. "As for me, once I fell in love, that was it."

"I believe you, but if I might add," Anne said, "So long as your wife lives, and loves you exclusively." Even in the case of her father, who had loved her mother dearly, Mr. Elliot had found a way to compartmentalize his feelings and go on with his life. Anne did not believe women were as fortunate.

"Perhaps you are right…" Harve mused.

Emboldened, Anne continued, "The main difference between men and women where love is involved, is that women love the longest…even when there seems to be no hope."

Anne paused, feeling as if her beating heart had been exposed for the world to see. She surprised herself by revealing these intimate thoughts to Harve. After the words left her mouth, Anne instantly felt quite vulnerable. She still loved Rick and would forever do so. Even now that all hope seemed gone, Anne would never be able to separate herself from the impact Rick had made on her life.

As Harve was about to make another comment the hotel door opened, announcing the arrival of Mary and Etta who had returned from their shopping excursion. Had the girls not been so preoccupied on their many purchases they might have noticed Anne's blushing face or the way Rick was frantically scribbling away at the desk.

"We're back!" Mary announced loudly.

"Oh good…Anne's here!" Etta exclaimed happily at spotting her. "Anne, I can't wait to show you the dress I bought for you. I think you're gonna love it! But first, do you mind if I make a really quick call to Chuck?"

Anne nodded affirmatively. Etta immediately punched in Chuck's number before scurrying off to the back bedroom for privacy.

"Sis," Mary wasted no time in gaining Anne's attention. "Look at these adorable matching outfits I got the boys," she said, holding up two sets of train-themed overalls. Anne smiled, imagining her nephews pretending to be railroad conductors in their new clothes.

As Harve looked on, it was evident the man was beginning to feel out of place as Mary rummaged through various bags to show off her purchases. "Well, Rick…" he said, moving towards his friend. "You about ready? I think the room has been reclaimed by the ladies."

Rick inclined his head as if in agreement, but seemed unnerved. When Rick made no effort to get up, Harve sent him a curious look. Rick cleared his throat, "Umm…I need a few more minutes."

"What are you writing, man, a novel!?!" Harve exclaimed, playfully punching Rick's shoulder.

Rick shook his head to deny the charge but semi-chuckled along with the others. "Sorry, it's just that I remembered something else I needed to jot down before I forgot it."

Anne sensed an oddly vulnerable state in Rick which was different from his normal behavior. Devoting more of her focus to study him, she noted that Rick didn't want Harve hovering over him. *What's going on?* she thought as she continued to watch with peaked curiosity at the interaction between the two men.

Harve grimaced teasingly as he glanced at the women gathered around their multiple purchases. "At this rate, I'll have to see every outfit!"

Although the rest of the party found this comment amusing, Rick didn't respond in kind. Instead he plowed ahead with his writing rather than allowing himself to be distracted by his friend. When Anne looked to Harve for his reaction, she was surprised at the concerned look he sent her. Harve found Rick's behavior troubling as well.

"I thought you'd be used to it by now," Clara said, claiming Harve's attention as she responded to his earlier jesting. "I understand Melissa can be quite the shopper herself."

"Alas, it is too true, her passion for home interiors never ceases to amaze me," he said as a defeated man, but his lament was accompanied with a twinkle in his eye.

Mary touched Anne's arm. "Do you think the boys might still fit into these by Christmas?" she asked, referring again to the outfits she had shown Anne upon her arrival.

Anne held them up for further inspection. "I'm not sure, Mary. You would know best."

Mary nodded, but Anne could tell she had been hoping for something a bit more concrete. Although Anne had a general inclination that they would, she didn't feel qualified to give a confident answer, not being around the boys enough to know their rate of growth.

Saving Anne from further questions, Rick captured everyone's attention when he finally rose from his chair. Grabbing the recently written papers which previously consumed his attention, Rick proceeded to fold one of the sheets in half. Harve took this as an indication his friend was now ready to leave and began moving towards the door.

"Well, looks like we're headin' out," Harve said to Clara, eager to leave behind all the chaos. "I bet you girls will appreciate some 'alone' time."

As Clara and Mary began to say their goodbyes, Anne's attention was redirected when she noticed Rick attempting to make eye contact with her. The gesture was far too obvious and pointed to be imagined, yet Anne felt it to be somehow surreal, like a dream. Rick's riveted and compelling look led her to see the note in his hand, which he then tucked under the leather table mat on the desk. Locking eyes with Anne once more, she couldn't mistake the pleading request Rick was making, which was confirmed by his tapping the mat directly over the now hidden message. Anne felt stunned, almost paralyzed, and yet a consuming urge beckoned her to rush directly to the note. *What could he have written?* Anne pondered.

"We'll see you later tonight at the Elliot's?" Clara's voice cut through the insanity surrounding Anne's mind.

Harve nodded and turned the door handle, only waiting long enough for Rick to catch up before leaving. All of this went unnoticed by Anne who's concentration was solely on the piece of paper and the telling look Rick gave her before his departure.

"Mom," Mary sought Clara's attention once the men were gone. "Etta and I spotted a dress for you to wear at the wedding."

"Really? Where at?" Clara asked, all ears since she'd been having trouble finding just the right outfit for this special occasion.

"Macy's," Mary responded without missing a beat. "It's the perfect color, and it has a matching jacket." Overjoyed, Clara listened as Mary proceeded to describe the dress in detail while Anne remained in her frozen state.

Cautiously looking to see if the women were paying any attention to her, Anne found them completely preoccupied. Taking a deep breath, Anne nervously inched her way to the desk—her desire and great anticipation driving her to see what Rick had written. *Is it good news or bad news?* Anne thought anxiously. *Did something I said earlier move him? Or maybe the opposite, and I inflamed his anger so much that he couldn't wait to express his disappointment in me?* Checking again to see if the girls were still engaged elsewhere, Anne quickly lifted the table mat ever so slightly and slid the folded piece of paper out from underneath, grasping it with concealed eagerness.

Feeling especially tense, Anne stole another glance in their direction. Mary, maintaining her domination of the conversation was now in the process of describing various shoes and accessories which could be purchased to complete Clara's perfect look. Before opening the note, Anne tried to compose herself. Recalling Rick's face just prior to his departure, she drew courage. Either way, Anne would cherish the unique intimacy just that little interaction with Rick had allowed her that afternoon. Anne knew the contents of the letter would bring one of two things: either fulfillment of her hopes, or the final blow that would shatter her heart into a million pieces.

Feeling like she couldn't wait another minute to see what the future held, Anne slowly began to unfold the letter with trembling hands. As she did so, it was almost as if the note whispered to her the promise of freedom—the freedom to love or to let go. Anne was ready—she was over seven years ready.

Inside was Rick's familiar hand writing scribbled across the page, and Anne felt her eyes glisten as she began to read the letter that would forever change her life. As she read the words became alive, and in her mind, she heard Rick's strong and masculine voice speaking.

My most dearest and lovely Anne,

I felt as if my life had ceased to exist when your family persuaded you not to marry me. Although I never stopped loving you, to my shame, I have to confess to also harboring feelings of resentment, bitterness, anger, and disappointment. Like a fool, I let my pride get involved, and stupidly walked away. I should have stayed to earn your dad's approval and make something of myself. Instead of putting your feelings first, all I worried about was my bruised ego and thought you'd surely come after me. But as days turned into months, and then months into years, I realized I'd been foolish and let down the most important person in my life. By then, so much time had elapsed, I began to believe it was too late to fix what we once shared. I was sure you'd forgotten me, and more than likely already married someone else. I convinced myself that what you had felt for me was merely a school girl's crush, and it was only I who had experienced real love. Yet, after hearing the words you spoke today, I dared to hope again.

Anne, I know in my heart we were meant to be together—everything within tells me that. Even still, I fear I am only fooling myself that you might feel the same way. But I must try once more—I won't let fear rule me. Anne, I offer once again my heart, my everything. But this time I do it as a grown man who loves you more than ever before. Do you remember the first time I asked for your hand on bended knee? It is a moment I will never forget. Please know that you have been my only love, and it is

233

a love I have held constant. You alone have the power to touch my heart and soul.

Anne forced herself to stop reading, overwhelmed by her surging emotions and finding it difficult to breathe. Sinking into the chair, Anne closed her eyes and tried to remind herself that this was no dream. The note before her was tangible and true, a testimony bearing one of the most beautiful love stories Anne had ever imagined—and surprisingly, it was hers. Glancing again to see if she was still unobserved, Anne resumed her reading.

You are the reason I came to California. Please trust and know that men can stay true, believe it of me—and know that it is only you of which I think of day and night.

Harve wants to go, so I hope to draw your attention to this letter. The next time I see you, just one look at your face—the face that has so fully captured my heart—it alone will tell me whether you are to be mine now and forever.

"Anne, here it is!" Etta announced, draping a flowing bridesmaid's dress in front of Anne.

Anne had not even heard Etta approach. Her emotions were already heightened from the letter, so the surprise of finding Etta upon her caused Anne to jump noticeably. Not wanting Rick's letter to be seen, Anne swiftly stuffed the note into her pocket where her trembling hand remained. But Anne could not so easily hide her shock-white complexion or shaken countenance. Although Anne tried to appear normal, her agitated state was far too obvious, drawing the attention of the women as they began scrutinizing Anne's odd behavior.

"Anne, are you alright?" Etta asked with concern. "Mom, come see how pale Anne is."

Clara advanced towards Anne for a closer inspection. "Why, Anne, you look like you've seen a ghost," Clara observed, kneeling next to her.

"Sis, are you feeling okay? You seem on edge," Mary remarked.

Anne found it difficult to speak. Clearing her throat, it took a moment before her vocal chords responded. "No... I...I need to go home," Anne uttered in a faint voice.

"Right now? You look too weak to walk!" Etta voiced incredulously.

"Be serious, Anne," Mary pressed.

"Yes!" Anne said with a little more gusto than she had intended. "Right away."

Anne got up and made a path across the room to retrieve her purse. She didn't want all this attention and needed some space to clear her thoughts, not a medical team trying to assess her physical status.

"Anne, you really should lie down," Clara suggested, showing her concern.

Before Anne could refuse, Charles entered with Little Charlie and Nicholas, each boy bounding towards their mother, eager to share about their exciting day with Daddy. Anne was grateful for their arrival, as it created a temporary diversion. Mary greeted both her boys with hugs.

"Mom! Guess what we saw!" Nicholas exclaimed animatedly. "An octopus!" He wiggled his hands to represent the sea creature's movement.

"My goodness!" she said with mock excitement.

"It had all these legs, and a worker let both of us touch one," Nicholas answered proudly.

"A live octopus?" Mary questioned her son, turning to Charles for confirmation while she held Nicholas' hands at bay.

"No, Mary, it was a dead one in a jar," Charles jested, knowing his wife's aversion to sea creatures.

"Charles!" Mary said peeved, "You know how I feel about the boys touching stuff like that!" She ushered both boys to the sink to thoroughly wash their hands.

"Mary, calm down," Charles replied, "A little sea juice won't harm them."

"Anne, would you like me to drive you?" Etta asked, turning everyone's attention back towards Anne. Etta had spotted Anne slowly inching her way to the door with her car keys in hand.

"Really, it's not necessary. I'm fine," Anne tried to say convincingly, hoping to not have Charles get involved as well—but with no such luck.

"Is everything alright?" he asked to Anne's dismay. Good gravy! All she wanted to do was slip out quietly without turning her departure into a full-blown fanfare.

"I'm sorry, it's just my nerves…I really need to go home," Anne said with determination, reaching for the door. "And Etta…the dress…I think it's perfect." Anne smiled kindly at all the concerned faces.

As if prodded by Clara's still anxious expression, Charles took a step towards her. "Are you sure you don't need someone to drive you home?"

"No, Charles," Anne said, turning the doorknob before stopping. "But…"

"Yes, Anne?" Charles answered quickly, hopeful that perhaps she had changed her mind.

"Could you please be sure to tell Harve and Rick that I hope to see them tonight at my house?" Anne asked.

"Sure, no problem," Charles replied, thinking her request odd.

"It's important," Anne urged pleadingly. "You won't forget, will you?"

"Harve told me himself he's planning on coming," Clara tried to put Anne at ease, "And I'm sure that means Rick will be there as well."

Anne thanked Clara then exited the room without further delay. Stepping inside the elevator, she punched the close button, unable to wait for the doors to shut on their own. Even still, the doors moved at what seemed like a snail's pace and Anne felt her impatience growing. "Dear God, please let this be for real," Anne prayed out loud, still trying to grasp what was happening.

To give herself assurance, Anne pulled out Rick's note from her pocket and read the words over again, only pausing when the elevator signaled it had reached the ground floor. Once the doors opened, Anne rushed out, making her way through the automated entrance doors of the hotel in pursuit of her vehicle.

"Anne!"

At hearing her name, Anne halted in her tracks. Either her mind was playing tricks on her, or it was the voice of her beloved. Her breath caught as she slowly turned to see him standing outside the hotel's entrance. Rick had waited for her—this wasn't a dream!

It was as if time stood still for them while they gazed at each other, both expressing in their look the unlimited love they were now ready to finally share. Anne felt her eyes begin to brim with tears as her happiness threatened to spill over. She was an emotional wreck, not knowing whether to laugh or cry—but when the first tear finally rolled down her cheek, Rick ran quickly to her and enveloped her in his strong arms.

"Anne, my precious Anne…" Rick said, kissing the top of her head.

In the comfort of his embrace, Anne felt overwhelmed with blissful gratitude, wishing this moment would never end.

He pulled back slightly in order to look directly at Anne. "I told myself I couldn't return to you until I was able to prove myself worthy of not only you, but also of your family," Rick spoke these words as he gently stroked her cheek. "I'm sorry I took so long."

Anne could no longer contain her emotions, and unrestrained tears came streaming down her face. "It was always my wish you'd come back," she whispered.

He squeezed her tightly. "You never forgot me?" he asked, his voice raw with emotion.

"No...never," Anne answered, cupping his face with her hands before he pulled her in close again. This time she nestled her head into Rick's chest shyly, breathing in his manly scent—hoping he'd never let her go again.

Chapter 45

Anne beamed as she made her way to her bedroom, closing the door behind her. She couldn't stop smiling. Rick still loved her! And to know he wanted to make her his wife, even planning to approach her father that very evening to seek her hand in marriage.

Getting a sudden urge to reminisce, Anne went to her hope chest. Opening it, she pulled out an old photo showing the two of them on one of their very first dates. She had to laugh at the sappy smiles on their youthful faces. It was evident they were in the throes of young puppy love, each having star dust in their eyes and dreaming of a future life together...dreams that amazingly would now come true.

Stroking the frame gently, Anne was overcome with these tender memories. Anne recalled the first time she saw Rick, and how he had rescued her. The time they gazed under a moonlit sky, making plans for their future. And then there was the gut-wrenching night when Rick walked away. The heartache Anne had experienced through that ordeal was devastating and life altering. But his recent letter had transformed everything. Their love seemed so much richer because of their past, and somehow the years spent apart had only made their love grow deeper. Time had matured them, allowing each to offer a more nurturing and stable love. Anne never would have wished for their separation, but loathe as she was to admit it, now realized it had been for the best.

The separation had only given the two of them more wisdom and life experience to better handle the responsibilities of married life. Because of it, Anne knew their future together would thrive and flourish. She felt an immense gratitude for this second chance and was blessed beyond measure.

Wiping her glistening eyes, Anne got up and walked to her vanity, propping the cherished photo against the mirror. As she did so, Anne caught a glimpse of herself and smiled at her reflection—she was glowing with renewed love.

Laughter filled the Elliot's home later that evening as the charity event was well underway. Money, food and drinks were flowing liberally, as well as the haughtiness Anne found so repulsive. Biding her time until Rick showed up, she found solace in the family room apart from the crowd, watching television and eating popcorn with Little Charlie and Nicholas now that her help was no longer needed. Every time her thoughts wandered to that of Rick, a big, silly grin lit up her already glowing face, prompting one of her nephews to ask what was making her so happy.

"Aunt Anne, why is your smile so big?" Little Charlie asked.

"Because I feel loved, Charlie," Anne responded, tucking his hair behind his ear.

"Yes, but I've never seen you smile this huge before," he mused, taking another bite of popcorn.

"You'll find out why soon," she said with a conspiratorial grin.

"Is it a secret?" Nicholas asked, joining in.

"Yes," Anne answered, wrapping her arms around the boys. "But I can't say anything more about it right now."

"But we can keep a secret—" Nicholas began to object as Elizabeth poked her head into the room.

"There you are, Anne!" the irritation rang in Elizabeth's voice. "We're all out of cherries. Do you know where they are?"

"Cupboard to the left of the sink, top shelf," Anne replied without hesitation. She remembered exactly where she'd placed the cherries after returning from the grocery store yesterday afternoon.

"Can't you get it?" Elizabeth looked aghast.

Anne sighed. "Of course," she said as she stood up, "I'm sorry, I thought you only wanted to know *where* they were. I didn't realize you expected me to get them."

Elizabeth sent her sister a snide look before leaving the room while Anne begrudgingly moved towards the kitchen. On her way, Anne peeked in on the gaming area with the hope that Rick might have arrived. To her disappointment he had not, but she spied Will in the process and he seemed quite eager to gain Anne's attention. Will sent her a cocky smile as he held up his winning collection of money chips, thinking it would impress her. Unfazed by his success, Anne only nodded a quick acknowledgment before turning on her heels, leaving Will rather disconcerted. He couldn't focus on the rest his game, wondering what could have triggered her cool behavior towards him. Folding his hand of poker and cashing in the rest of his chips, Will decided to find out.

As he was exiting the room, Will noticed Rick just arriving, and it was obvious Wentworth was searching the area, no doubt for Anne. Will found himself beyond irritated by this man's annoying existence. Out of spite, Will chose to change his route in order to "accidentally" knock shoulders with Rick to assert his manhood. Rick brushed off the juvenile challenge, but made sure Will understood through an unmistakable look he would brook no further stunts of this nature. During this interchange, Rick became aware that Will was not the only one who seemed to find his arrival distasteful.

Eyeing Wentworth, Mr. Elliot turned to Elizabeth who was playing Yahtzee with him at one of the tables. "There's that man again!" Mr. Elliot commented, releasing his roll and watching the dice come to a stop just one sequence short of a full house. "Who is *he* anyway?" Walter continued with even more irritation. "I certainly didn't invite him. Do you think we should ask him to leave?"

Elizabeth glanced back at Rick and observed how Wentworth seemed to be in search of someone. She tried to flag him over to their table, but he didn't seem to notice. "I told you the other night, Dad. That's Rick Wentworth and I don't think you'll want him to leave. I did some research on him the other night and discovered he's actually a rather celebrated and wealthy author. Apparently even Hollywood is starting to take notice of his books."

"Really?" Mr. Elliot's scowl transformed into an interested smile. "Well, this event *is* for a good cause. I guess it won't hurt for him to stay."

Back in the kitchen, Anne quickly located the maraschino cherries exactly where she told Elizabeth they would be.

"That wasn't difficult," she mumbled to herself as she set the jar down on the countertop to search for an appropriate serving dish in which to display them. Anne found a small silver bowl in the shape of a leaf and thought it'd be perfect for the job.

Giving the lid a few taps on the counter, Anne attempted to open the jar, but the seal refused to budge. Applying more pressure, Anne felt her hand begin to burn as she struggled further to pry it loose. She was just about to place the lid under hot water when Anne felt the jar being taken out of her hands. Startled, she lurched backwards only to find arms steadying her. Letting out a little shriek, Anne looked up to see that it was only Will.

"Will!" she exclaimed out of breath, "You came out of nowhere!" Anne placed her hand to her heart to calm herself.

Will chuckled, and with little effort on his part succeeded in opening the jar, handing it back to her. "A bit jumpy, eh?" he said with a smirk.

Anne ignored the comment but thanked him. She didn't want to disclose that it was actually him which made her "jumpy". Attempting to avoid further eye contact, Anne began transferring the cherries from the jar into the decorative bowl. While bent on this task, she became aware that Will had moved closer to her.

Wasting no time, Will's lips brushed her ear as he began to whisper, "Did you think some more about what I asked?" he said with a sultry voice.

"About what?" Anne asked, the hairs on the back of her neck standing up as she cringed at Will's nearness.

Without warning, Will grasped one of her shoulders, turning her to face him, then placed his other hand around her waist. Anne felt paralyzed in his embrace. "About me…" Will continued, "…about me loving and pampering you all the days of your life."

In a state of shock, Anne tried to pull away from Will, but his strength was overpowering. "Will, let me go!" she entreated. But before Anne knew it, his lips were on a collision course with hers. Maneuvering her face away just in time, Will planted a big juicy kiss on Anne's cheek, and it was wet. "Will, stop!" Anne squirmed, which only caused him to hold her more tightly.

"Excuse me," the steely sound of Rick's masculine voice demanded attention, causing Will to freeze.

For Anne, the voice, no matter how steely, was ever so welcome. Giving Rick a brilliant smile, Anne was able to communicate to him the instant joy and relief she felt at seeing him.

Opposite Anne, Will's sour expression showed just how infuriated he was by Wentworth's intrusion. "Look…*Ralph* is it?" Will began condescendingly.

"It's Rick," Wentworth corrected him.

"Whatever. Anyway, as you can see, you have rather *bad timing*. Do you mind?"

"Actually, I do mind," Rick said, taking a step closer as Will shrunk back. "And, unlike you, I think my timing is impeccable." Rick flexed his hand until his knuckles turned white. "A moment later, and it would have been necessary for me to beat the living daylights out of you."

"You wouldn't dare," Will threatened.

"Actually, I would," Rick didn't back down, "You see, I don't particularly appreciate another man touching my fiancé."

Will's eyes bugged out as he glanced back and forth between Anne and Rick. "Your fiancé?" his once deep voice squeaked. "How come I didn't know about this?!"

Rick raised an eyebrow. "Well you're quite aware of it now, so please kindly take your hands off of Anne."

Will immediately complied, realizing Rick was not one to mess with. Finally free, Anne rubbed her sore arms as she moved to Rick, finding safety by his side.

Having overheard raised voices from the other room, Mr. Elliot and Elizabeth choose to investigate. "Will! What in heaven's name is going on in here?" Mr. Elliot demanded, embarrassed by the ruckus at his charity event.

"They're engaged!" Will exclaimed, pointing an accusatory finger at the happy couple. "That's what's going on in here!"

To Anne, Will looked like a child who hadn't gotten his way and was tattling to her dad—it was disturbing to say the least. But to Will's bitter disappointment, instead of looking shocked and disgusted, Mr. Elliot seemed pleasantly surprised.

"Really? Engaged?" Walter asked, turning to Anne for confirmation. "Anne? Is this true?" Without hesitation, Anne answered her father with an instant smile and an affirmative nod. Walter, wanting further clarification asked, "...to be married?" and Anne once again smiled.

"That is, with your blessing, sir," Rick added respectfully.

Anne peered over at Elizabeth who was standing silently in the background, her face exhibiting a raging battlefield of pain, regret and anger. Anne felt pity for her sister at seeing the bitter tears stream down her cheeks. Elizabeth had always thought she'd be the first to get married. After all, she was the prettiest, wasn't she? And the favorite? What right did her younger sister, the one Elizabeth had secretly been jealous of, to get married before herself? And worse of all, to a man like Rick who had it all—looks, status, and *money*.

Mr. Elliot turned around to consult with Elizabeth. "How much did you say he was worth, again?" he asked in a low voice, though not so low that Anne couldn't hear.

"Millions, Dad, literally millions," Elizabeth hissed through clenched teeth, her voice filled with raw jealousy.

Mr. Elliot turned around again to face the couple, extending his hand towards Rick, adding with a huge smile, "Welcome to the family, *son.*"

Chapter 46

The day had finally arrived. In less than an hour, Anne would officially be Mrs. Rick Wentworth. The dream she'd held onto for the past seven and a half years had not been in vain. Even though the time spent apart had been long, strangely it seemed as if they had never been separated. Anne was amazed at how they'd been able to pick right up from where they had left off, and fortunately this time, much more prepared to meet whatever tomorrow would bring.

The past three months of planning their wedding had been a complete joy for the couple as they came together to make their special day unforgettable. Not wanting anything too elaborate, they chose a simple but timeless old church in the eastern hills of California overlooking the picturesque and scenic vineyards.

Flying in the week before, Carol worked alongside Anne to bring about all her god-daughter had envisioned, turning Anne's ideas into reality. The two transformed the chapel, infusing it with soft lighting while incorporating white veil netting that swooped between the banisters lining the aisles. The final touch was the floral arch, decorated with a string of lights where the couple would exchange their vows. The sanctuary had turned out even more magical than Anne dreamed possible.

And now, Anne stood in the Sunday school room with the glow of the afternoon sun reflecting off her mother's white

Kaitlin Saunders

wedding gown. Soon, Anne would walk the long aisle to be joined with her groom. Instead of fear, Anne was filled with eagerness to finally make a lifelong covenant with the one she wanted to spend forever with. There were no doubts for Anne, only happiness knowing with Rick by her side, it would be an unforgettable adventure.

Looking in the full length mirror, Anne viewed the exquisite gown with its flowy train and sheer lace veil that covered her face. Although Anne's mother's dress incorporated simple lines, it radiated elegance and class. It meant so much to be able to include the memory of her mom on this day. As Anne fingered the small, precious Bible which had also belonged to Emma, she silently thanked God for all her blessings.

Inside the Bible was Rick's letter, used as a bookmarker for the passage in First Corinthians 13, the section Anne planned on reading to Rick during their vows. It read:

Love is patient and kind; love does not envy or boast; it is not arrogant or rude. It does not insist on its own way; it is not irritable or resentful; it does not rejoice at wrongdoing, but rejoices with the truth. Love bears all things, believes all things, hopes all things, endures all things.

Hearing a knock at the door, Anne turned to see a moist-eyed Carol peeking inside. "Dear, it's time," she said with a motherly smile.

Once Carol had personally witnessed the love and dedication the couple shared for each other, she embraced their engagement wholeheartedly. Yet Carol's happiness was dimmed with the regret at being partially responsible for having separated them in the past. Anne, however, was quick to reassure her friend that everything happens for a reason, adding she and Rick had needed the time apart to truly be ready for the plans God had in store for them. These words helped to ease her godmother's mind, and when Anne asked

Carol to stand in her mother's place by lighting the unity candle alongside Rick's sister during the ceremony, she wept with joy. It was an honor Carol did not take lightly.

With one final look in the mirror, Anne walked with her godmother to the church's foyer where Mr. Elliot was waiting anxiously. Walter's breath caught at the sight of his daughter dressed in white.

"Anne, you look beautiful," her father choked out with emotion. "You remind me so of your mother."

Anne was touched by this rare display of affection, and felt her eyes begin to glisten. Taking her dad's arm, Anne kissed him softly on the cheek while Walter wiped away a stray tear at the corner of his eye.

Carol gave Anne a final hug just before taking the usher's arm to disappear behind the closed doors. Anne moved forward, and as she did so could hear the music she and Rick selected for their wedding. The next song to play would be "Unforgettable" by Nat King Cole, knowing it was her cue to enter.

As the romantic tune began to sound, the double doors opened, and the crowd stood in respect of the approaching bride. Anne shared a special smile with her father before Walter began to proudly escort her down the aisle to the man who would soon be her husband, the man she loved with all her heart...

Epilogue

Safely inside the back seat of their chauffeured car, the new-lyweds stole a kiss as the driver began to pull away from the church and all its fanfare. Anne turned to wave at her family and friends, grateful for their attendance. She continued to wave as the limo neared the end of the drive, at which point Rick took his wife's hand to hold it gently.

Gazing tenderly into her eyes Rick spoke softly, "Well, Mrs. Wentworth," causing Anne to smile at hearing her new name, "You've quite outdone yourself today, my lady..." Anne's pulse quickened as Rick leaned in and kissed her neck, moving his lips up to her ear and whispering, "...by making me the happiest man in the world."

With their eyes locked in mutual admiration, Anne placed her hand tenderly on Rick's cheek, stroking his chin softly. "...and I, the luckiest woman," she answered, sealing their love with a kiss.

THE END